Grayton Beach Dreams

Grayton Beach Dreams

Love Along Hwy 30A
Book Five

Melissa Chambers

Also by Melissa Chambers

Love Along Hwy 30A Series:
Seaside Sweets
Seacrest Sunsets
Seagrove Secrets
WaterColor Wishes

Young Adult titles:
The Summer Before Forever (Before Forever #1)
Falling for Forever (Before Forever #2)
Courting Carlyn (Standalone)

For all my beautiful friends in their forties who help make Cassidy's character realistic

Chapter One

The offer on the table was one Cassidy had trouble refusing—not because it was such an attractive offer, but because her chest panged with guilt. She needed to do more. Dedicating two months a year to helping people in Jamaica or wherever the efforts were currently focused was a drop in the bucket compared to what she could be doing. But as much as she hated to admit it, her comfortable home in Seaside, Florida was her sanctuary.

She folded her arms over her chest, scanning the pink and aqua walls and floors of her bakery. Her stomach soured just thinking about her friends from her volunteer group making food for hungry children while she served cinnamon rolls and muffins to privileged vacationers. Those people dedicated their lives to that work. Cassidy committed to two months a year, some years. But now, with Todd's offer, she had the chance to go and help full-time…devote her life to the greater good. She just wasn't sure she had it in her. She was damn sure no saint.

Todd had been lovely. That was the word for it. He was a solid man. Considerate, kind, funny at times, and possessing a heart of gold...mostly. He had his faults, as everyone did. He could at times be a little self-important, but she almost felt guilty thinking that about him. The man had devoted his life to helping people. So what if he did it on his terms. He was a man. They mostly did things on their terms.

The bell on her bakery's door dinged, getting her attention. Bo Harrison walked toward her with that guilty grin of his, glancing down at his shoes and then back up at her. She was fairly sure she hadn't seen him without Maya on his arm since the two of them found their way to one another last, what, May? June?

As he approached the counter, her core ignited as it did every time she saw him. In her defense, she'd never seen a man ooze sexuality like Bo Harrison. It hadn't been that long ago that he was knocking on her door. Shooting him down had been a necessary evil. Guys like Bo, before they met *the one* of course, were in it for the sex. In her case, he'd probably had some misguided cougar fantasy he'd wanted to live out.

Cassidy never understood the attraction of the one-night-stand. For her, sex was about furthering a connection that was established through mutual admiration and respect...deepening emotions that were built on trust. A night with Bo would have been like eating a hot fudge sundae—sinfully delicious going down, but marked with immediate regret. They shared the same friends. She didn't want to have to wear red cheeks every time she saw him at a gathering, not to mention the rumors that would have gone around this chatty group of hers. No thanks. She had a vibrator that worked just fine.

She met him with a smile. "I was expecting your wife."

"Sorry to disappoint you with the worse half."

"How is your lovely bride?"

"She's awesome." Bo went pink-cheeked, grinning from ear to ear. His smile infected Cassidy, filling her chest with warmth. She had turned him down on several occasions, even punching him in the nose once when he'd had way too much to drink and tried to kiss her. But she couldn't deny that he deserved the love he'd received from Maya. He'd had a rough go of it in his twenties getting tied up in a long-term relationship that was littered with addiction on the woman's part. Maya was a beautiful soul, and Bo was a complete man with her.

Cassidy gave him her warmest smile. "I'm truly happy for you, Bo."

Somehow his grin grew a few inches. "Thanks." He scratched his head. "And, uh, I want to apologize if I ever made you uncomfortable with my advances." He met her gaze with an innocence she never knew he had in him. He was always so full of bravado and confidence, but clearly the love of a wonderful woman had humbled him.

It was moments like this she was so thankful she'd never caved and let herself fall for him. It'd taken strength beyond her capabilities at times, because as much as she wanted sex to be about connection, those connections had come few and far between in her time. She had primal needs that went unmet on an ongoing basis. And God knew if any man could have filled them, it would have been him.

But she'd been worried she'd fall for him or, worse, he'd fall for her. Bo was in his mid-thirties. Those were the baby-making years. Those days were in Cassidy's rearview. As much as she enjoyed children—her nephew Daryl's boys were her favorite humans on earth—she'd never had the urge to have her own. She considered fostering an older child one day, possibly, but bearing a child wasn't in her plans. The last thing she ever wanted was to handcuff a younger man into a relationship with her, keeping him from having his own children and being filled with regret a decade later, saddled with a fifty-something-year-old woman.

"You were always respectful, Bo," she said.

They pointed at each other and said in unison, "Except that one time."

He winced. "I'm sorry about that."

"You've apologized many times for that night. Once was plenty."

"There was no coming back from that, was there?" he asked.

She shook her head. "Probably not. It would have been hard to kiss a man I'd previously punched."

He nodded, his face and neck seeping red. God, he was embarrassing her with his own humiliation. She wondered if being on a straight and narrow road with Maya had made him look back on past regrets.

She saved them both from any further conversation on the subject by fetching the cake

Maya had ordered. "Here you go. I hope your nephew has a wonderful birthday." Bo pulled out his wallet and she held up a hand. "Maya already paid in advance," she lied. She'd never felt right about taking money from friends.

He frowned. "You sure? She told me she hadn't."

Cassidy waved him off. "Oh yeah. She probably forgot." She came from around the counter to walk him to the door so she could lock it behind him. It was close enough to quitting time. When they got to the door, she went to open it, and he went to hug her all at the same time, leaving them in an awkward limbo. After a few attempts at him opening the door and her trying to hug back, they both stopped and looked at each other with smiles.

He held out his free arm. "Can I have a hug?"

She smiled for him. "Of course."

They hugged, and then she let him go and opened the door. "So good to see you, Bo. Please tell Maya hello."

"I will. She wants to have a dinner party at the house with all the group in a couple of weeks. I hope you'll come. I know you pick and choose your occasions to get out."

"I'll make it for sure. Just let me know when."

"Will do," he said with his million-dollar grin.

They both turned to find a guy with auburn-ish, shaggy hair on the sidewalk in front of them. Jesse, the bartender and owner of the Bohemian Guppy in Grayton, who could single-handedly heat up South Walton. Marigold had introduced them last week at Cassidy's welcome back party, but Cassidy had seen him around. He was a full-on, unapologetic player.

Trouble coming and going. He'd hit on her that night, and she'd had a moment where she considered breaking her no-one-night-stand rule. But she'd stayed strong, thank God.

Jesse blinked when he took in Bo. "Hey man. Good to see you the other night at the bar."

Bo transferred the cake to his left arm and shook Jesse's hand. "What the hell are you doing here?" Bo asked.

"I'm here to see Cassidy."

Bo lifted his eyebrows. "Oh, okay. Y'all know each other?"

Jesse met Cassidy's gaze with piercing blue eyes that put Bradley Cooper's to shame. He nodded at her. "We've met."

The three of them stood in a silent triangle, Jesse looking at Cassidy, and Bo glancing between them with curiosity. Cassidy didn't get embarrassed often, but something about standing with the door propped behind her in this confined space with two of the hottest guys in the Florida panhandle was making her squirm.

"You and Blake used to come in quite a bit," Jesse said. "What happened to the two of you?"

"Both got married," Bo said, taking the cake with this right hand and holding up his left, wedding ring on display.

"Ah," Jesse said, nodding as if someone had died. "Hey, you've still got your shop there in PCB?"

"Still running."

"Do you sell paddleboards? Mine's about bit the dust."

"Got a big selection of them. Come on in. I'll give

you the friends and family discount."

"Awesome. Thanks, man."

"Good to see you," Bo said, and then turned to Cassidy. "I'll see you soon, for that dinner."

"Absolutely," Cassidy said. Bo gave one more significant look between the two of them, almost like a concerned dad, and then he was off. Cassidy couldn't help a smile. She turned to Jesse. "Come on in."

Jesse came through the doorway. "I hope this isn't a bad time. Did I run him off?"

"No, he was just leaving. I suppose you're here to talk cookies?" she asked. They'd spoken briefly at his bar last week about the idea of putting a cookie on the menu. She was ready to hurry this along. Not that she didn't enjoy the visual man candy, but Jesse made her body feel things it really shouldn't at her place of business.

"Yeah," he said, seeming to wake up. "Cookies. I'm thinking about adding them to the menu."

She pulled back a chair at a table. "Have a seat. Can I get you anything? Coffee? A soda?"

"No, I'm fine." He sat. "Your friend Marigold gave me the idea a while back. She said I needed to serve cookies on my menu. Something sweet that wasn't an elaborate dessert. Something noncommittal that customers can snack on while they drink. Most of my customers are guys, and they don't tend to want dessert, so I've not really pursued it, but I want to bring more women into the bar, so I'd love to have something unique to entice them."

All this guy needed to do was stand in the doorway if he wanted to entice women into his bar.

"You think cookies will do the trick?" she asked.

"Marigold said they needed really good cookies." He formed a circle with what looked like strong, capable hands. "Big and thick, and warm."

Jesus Christ, she was going to have to dust off her vibrator when she got home. She cleared her throat, brushing her wild hair out of her face. She'd put the mess up in a knot earlier, but it basically had a life of its own. "What kinds of cookies?"

He made a motion with his hands like he was wiping a slate clean. "Chocolate chip. That's what Marigold said. Oozing with dark chocolate. No nuts. I'd heat them up for a few seconds on the grill before serving, so maybe they wouldn't even be all the way cooked. I'd keep them refrigerated, of course. I'm not sure how all this would work. Probably be a trial and error thing."

She nodded, thinking it through. "We could try that. A thick cookie partially baked. Or I could just provide you with the dough separated into balls." She should probably tell him there were about a million places that would sell him such a thing in bulk, but she wouldn't mind the business. "Would this be a standing order?"

"Yes, if it works out. Marigold said it was important these be fresh. I could come get them from you each day, or every other day, or whatever." His cheeks colored just a tad, making her core light up for some stupid reason.

Dammit, she was not interested in this man boy. How old was he anyway? Twenty-five? Surely he didn't own a bar in this expensive area at only twenty-five. If he did, he probably had help from his parents, which was a whole other issue. The last thing she needed was to take on some boy toy as a sugar mama. She had enough problems keeping the shop afloat and living a comfortable life in her overpriced home. She didn't need some kid latching onto her when Daddy's money ran out, if that was his game. God, it probably wasn't. Where had all that come from?

She was losing it, and she had a feeling it was because this guy was stoking a fire that had been lit in her for too long. She and Todd had one night of comfortable, passionless sex in Jamaica. It'd been fine. Adequate. She'd wrapped her arms around his thick belly and avoided running her fingers through his balding hair for fear of taking out the last remaining pieces. She cringed when she thought about what happened the second and final time they tried to do it.

But here Jesse sat in front of her with a full head of thick hair and muscled, tattooed arms. No belly to speak of. It'd been so long since she'd had a guy like this that she'd almost forgotten what it was like.

"Don't you think?" he asked.

"Hmm? Oh, yes, warm cookies are the best ones."

He smiled. "I asked if you thought I should offer vanilla ice cream on top."

She was zoning out now in a one-on-one conversation. What the hell was wrong with her? "Absolutely. But I'd suggest the menu item being the single cookie with the offer of ice cream for an extra charge. That way it keeps the non-committal aspect of the single, easy-to-eat cookie intact."

"I was thinking the exact same thing."

"Great. I'll get started on some samples this afternoon." She smiled at him and then stood.

He hesitated to stand. "Do you want to talk pricing?"

She waved him off. "Let me get into it and see if I can even provide you with a decent product. Once we get there, I'll put that together for you."

"Sounds good." He headed toward the door, but slowly. He needed to leave…just walk out the door. She was, for some odd reason, feeling a little vulnerable. Maybe it was seeing Bo and how he acknowledged his pursuit of her. Maybe it was the fact that she'd not smelled a young man like this up close since the George W. Bush administration. Or maybe it was the fact that this particular man made the temperature in her shop jump a few degrees.

He turned back toward her. "You should come by for a drink after you're done here. When do you close?"

"Five o'clock. I'm gonna lock up behind you."

"That's when I'm walking into my bar," he said. "Ships passing in the night, you and I are." He scrunched up his face like he was embarrassed of his words and shook his head, walking toward the door. He stopped. "Oh, here." He pulled a card out of his wallet and handed it to her. "Please call when you have that sample ready. I'll come get it, or you can come by and have a drink or whatever."

She took the card and tapped it against her hand. "I'll do that."

"Or, I'm usually there opening around eleven. You're welcome to stop by then if that works better."

"That would be good. I'm usually too exhausted

by five to move."

He smiled, his boyish charm in direct contrast with what she knew to be his full-on player personality on the inside. "See you soon."

"Yep," she said. He just needed to freaking leave before she did something really stupid, like take him up on that drink.

He headed out the door and she locked it up tight behind him. She walked straight to the back room and collapsed in the desk chair by her computer. "Jesus Christ, Cassidy," she said to herself. "Get a freaking grip."

She pulled up a search for chocolate chip cookie recipes. As the pages of cookie porn passed by her on the screen, all she could think about was that longish hair of Jesse's that would feel so good between her fingers.

Cassidy typically dated older men. She didn't seek them out, but it seemed to work out that way. Most of the single men her age were divorced with school-aged children or teenagers, and that just wasn't a road she was willing to travel down. If she'd wanted kids, she'd have had her own.

Older men were her safest bet. They challenged her intellectually...usually...sometimes. They did appreciate her body. She was good about keeping thin, though it'd gotten tougher as she'd aged. Lean Cuisine was her BFF, but that was mainly because she was too exhausted at the end of the day to cook something. Working as a baker didn't help matters, but she found being around the stuff all day long made her sort of impervious to it.

The older men she dated liked sex, but it was on a

schedule, timed out with their erectile dysfunction medication. They all hid it at first, taking it before their dates with her, but she'd learned the signs. Red neck, literally. The stuff doubled their body temperatures. She'd be sitting across from a man at dinner and he'd be eyeing her like a filet mignon. If she wasn't ready yet, she couldn't help feeling a little guilty for saying goodnight at the end of the meal and excusing herself, knowing he'd just prepped for the night out of hope. The medicine took the spontaneity out of sex. But she couldn't complain. She was starting to experience hot flashes and hair in places it'd never popped up before. Aging wasn't for sissies.

She imagined that Jesse did not need a pill to get a hard-on. He could probably have sex on command, just give him thirty seconds to think about boobs and he'd be there. She clucked her tongue against her cheek, shaking her head at herself. How old was she, anyway? Physically, her forties, mentally about twenty-two. And her mental self couldn't help but daydream about a night with Jesse.

Chapter Two

Two ships passing in the night. What the hell was he, the captain of the Love Boat?

Gracie strolled past Jesse in her underwear and a tank top, headed to the kitchen.

"Hey, what's that guy's name who's the captain on that old *Love Boat* show we've been watching?" he asked her.

She crunched on a carrot stick. "Captain Stubing."

That's who he was. Captain Stubing. Jesse, who had once talked three extremely attractive girls into a foursome starring him, told Cassidy Anderson of Seaside Sweets that they were ships passing in the night. He winced again at his idiocy.

Jesse had thought about little other the past four days than Cassidy Anderson. Ever since the night Marigold had introduced him to her, he'd been smitten. He'd come on way too strong, but that approach typically worked. Not with her though.

She'd just given him that look like he was a silly little boy and walked away, never giving him another look the rest of the night.

He'd spent the remainder of the evening eyeing her from behind the bar, but he'd not seen her look up at him a single time. He pulled back and took the all-business approach at her shop the other day, but she'd not seemed a bit interested, dismissing him like yesterday's news when they'd finished their business talk. Jesse wasn't used to this behavior from women. It'd been the rare occasion that he'd gone for a woman who'd been this disinterested in him. Sure, there was an age difference, but he was more attracted to this woman than any twenty-something girl who'd been in his bar in years.

Gracie walked into the living room with the bag of carrots in hand and plopped down on the couch beside him. She gauged him as she chewed. "Do you want to have sex?"

He looked up from his phone, perplexed. "I thought we weren't going to do that anymore."

"We're not. I mean, not regularly. Just once. I swear I won't get weird on you or anything."

"You've never gotten weird on me."

She pointed a carrot at him. "Exactly. I'm just so damned lonely."

"Uh, hello. I'm in the room."

"I'm starved then, for male affection. It's been like six weeks."

He went back to his phone, hoping if he ignored her she'd go away. Not that he wouldn't mind having sex, but he wasn't feeling it right then, not with her, at least. He loved Gracie, but living with her had made her feel more like a sister than someone to screw.

"What about you?" She nodded toward his bedroom. "I haven't heard you in there with a girl in a while. When was your last time?"

"I don't know," he said. He really didn't. How long had it been? Longer than usual for sure. He'd just not been into the game lately.

She set her bag of carrots down and straddled him, pulling his hair out of his face. "Why didn't we work out? Wanna give it another go?" He just rested his head back and stared at her. She wasn't expecting an answer. She leaned forward like she was going to kiss him, but instead face-planted into the couch cushion behind him. "Ugh! I just want a decent man. Is that too much to ask?"

He lifted her off of him and set her on the couch. "We've been over this. You're beautiful. You just pick the wrong guys."

"Like you?"

"Definitely like me. You deserve way better than that."

She let out a sigh, tilting her head against the couch cushion staring at him. "You're right to reject me. Sex would just complicate this relationship, and I need one thing to be working in my life right now." She eyed him. "So are you rejecting me because you want our friendship to survive, or is it some other reason?" She sniffed her armpit. "I don't stink, do I? I took a shower last night when we got home."

"You don't stink." He rested back on the couch, closing his eyes.

She grasped his knee. "Hang on. Are you seeing

someone?"

"No. Who would I be seeing?"

"You want to see someone, though, don't you?" He remained silent, crossing his arms over his chest. "Who?" she asked, with a hint of urgency in her voice. She shook him. "Jesse, who the fuck?"

He opened his eyes. "Nobody. Shit."

"It's somebody, because I haven't offered myself to you in about six months, and I look damn good right now. Have you taken a look at my ass lately? Barre, baby."

He let out a hard breath. He liked Gracie, but she was twenty-three...a young twenty-three. They'd had plenty of fun together, in bed and out of it, but he craved something more out of both a friend and a girlfriend. Damn, did he just use the "G" word?

"Your ass is beautiful, Gracie."

"Who is it?"

"Why do you care? You don't know her."

"Is she local?"

He gave her a look. "If she wasn't I'd have already sealed the deal and moved on."

She rubbed her hands together. "Ooh, a local chick. Let me live vicariously through you. Where does she work? Or is she one of these rich housewives who don't work?"

This was all-wrong. Cassidy was a beautiful, thoughtful, intelligent woman full of life experience and short on tolerance for bullshit, he guessed. The last thing he wanted was to be discussing his interest in her with Gracie, who while sweet and well-intentioned, was Cassidy's polar opposite in every way, even physically. Gracie was five feet tall and a hundred pounds soaking wet, and Cassidy had to be at least 5'10.

He got up. "I'm getting in the shower."

"If you want some company, let me know."

Now she was just stoking him like a fire. She had no intention of following through on that offer. He ought to take her up on it, just to see, but he wasn't in the mood in case she accepted.

But he certainly wouldn't turn Cassidy down. It wasn't his thing to go for older women, but something about Cassidy interested him on a level he hadn't experienced in a while. She had this way of looking at him that cut through all the bullshit…like she could see right through him. The idea both thrilled and terrified him. But most of all, it challenged him.

He showered and then headed to his bedroom and dressed for work. Checking himself in the mirror, he ran his fingers through his hair. He'd be thirty this year, and it was starting to show in his eyes. He'd been dreading turning thirty, but he couldn't really pinpoint why. He could, actually, he just didn't want to.

He shook off the past, just like he did any time he felt it creeping back in. He lived his life for the present. Looking back was futile and ineffectual. Right now, he was living his best life. His bar was doing well. He was fit and healthy. He looked good and he felt good. What more could he possibly ask for?

He pocketed his phone and wallet and grabbed his keys. "I'm out!" he shouted in the direction of Gracie's bedroom as he passed by but got no response. She'd figure it out.

He locked the front door behind him and hopped down the stairwell, through the small hallway, and then opened the back door to his bar. The clanging of pots and pans and voices of Juan and Stevie giving each other shit indicated all was well and moving forward for the day in the kitchen. If his line cooks were there for the day, he could deal with anything else. But Kelly coming out of the ladies room tying her apron around her waist indicated no major call-outs today. Life was good.

He headed behind the bar where he was most comfortable, checking that all was left in working order last night. He counted the register down like he did every morning, and then headed to his office to pull the bank bag out of the safe.

Closing the office door behind him, he stopped in his tracks as Cassidy Anderson stepped into his bar, glancing around, presumably looking for him. Her long wavy hair hung down over her bare shoulders, thanks to her thin-strapped tank top that she wore tucked into a pair of tattered jeans, a big, sort of rustic buckle on her belt. Fuck, was she wearing a bra? He didn't see any straps. He swallowed hard, instructing his cock to stay down, and headed that way.

When she met his gaze, she smiled like they were old friends getting ready to settle in for a catch-up. He wondered how she could make him feel so special without saying a word.

His instinct was to hug her, but as he approached her she handed him a glass dish. "I've been playing around. See what you think."

He took the dish, his body adjusting to the

letdown of not getting to touch her. "Great. Thanks."

"I think a turn in the skillet for a quick couple of minutes will achieve the goal. Marigold and I only tested about thirty or forty of them for quality control." She smiled at him, resting her slim fingers against her flat stomach just above that belt buckle.

"Thanks for taking one for the team," he said.

"No problem." She glanced around his bar for a quick minute while he fumbled for words to keep the conversation going. She moved toward the door. "Let me know if you'd like to take next steps."

Just as she was walking away, he found his voice. "Yes, I definitely would."

Her eyebrows went up.

"I'm ready…for the next steps, that is," he said.

"Would you like to test them out first?"

"Nah. I trust you…and Marigold."

She shrugged. "Okay, then. Is now a good time to work out details?"

"Yes, it is." He indicated a chair at an empty table. "Have a seat. Would you like a drink?"

"Oh, um," she said, looking in the direction of the bar, "I think I'm okay."

"I've got a new berry sour beer on tap I'd love to get your opinion on. Do you like sour beer?"

She met his gaze, a gleam in her eye. "I love sour beer. Nobody ever has it on tap."

God he was glad he'd fallen for that sales pitch from that local brewer. "Sit. I'll be right there." He set the dish and the bank bag down on the table and then headed behind the bar. He returned with two cups of the sour beer and sat across from her.

She pointed at the bank bag. "You just left me

with an unlocked bank bag."

"Did you steal any money from me?"

"I may have. You better recount it all."

He smiled. "You wouldn't do that to me."

She sat back in her chair, her hair falling against the freckled skin on her chest. "How do you know what I'd do to you, Jesse?"

His body ignited with heat. This was the moment where he'd typically give it right back to the girl and go in for the close, but he somehow found himself fumbling for words. He messed with the zipper on the bank bag. "I guess I don't know, do I?" Holy fuck what was wrong with him? He inwardly coached himself. *You can do this. Get back on the bicycle, you idiot.*

"Do you have a figure in mind?" she asked.

Hell yes he had her figure in mind. "Um…"

"What's your planned price point?"

Heat seeped into his neck as he glanced up at her. Cookies. They were talking about fucking cookies, he reminded himself. "I was thinking maybe two-fifty? Two-ninety-nine?"

She lifted her cup. "I'd go at least two-ninety-nine. An extra dollar ninety-nine to make it a la mode." She paused before putting the cup to her lips. "That's just my suggestion. You may have other ideas."

God, did he have ideas…ones that would keep the two of them in bed for days. "That sounds right."

"If you went with a two-ninety-nine price point, I wouldn't feel so bad about charging you a buck fifty per cookie, plus delivery fees."

"I can come get them in the mornings. My bank is

in Seaside. I come that way most mornings to make the deposit anyway."

"And you've never stopped in for a muffin before. Shame on you."

With every word out of this woman's mouth, Jesse had to struggle harder to keep his cock at bay.

"When would you like me to start?" she asked.

Right fucking now. He pointed at the dish. "I'll use these for samples today. I'll take a dozen for tomorrow, if you can do it?"

"I most definitely can." She stood from the table, and he hoped he could without embarrassment.

"Let me cut you a check," he said.

She waved him off. "Pay me in a week or two. We'll see how this goes."

"Okay," he said. He walked her to the door, trying hard not to stare at her heart-shaped ass in those jeans.

She turned back toward him. "I'll see you in the morning."

"Is about this time okay?" he asked.

She gave him that same smile as when she first walked in—the one that made him feel like a king. "It's perfect." She headed down the street, pulling her keys out of her pocket.

God what he'd do to her if she'd let him.

He turned around to find Kelly in his face holding the bank bag. "You left this unattended on that table."

"Nobody's in here yet," he said, noticing a few people at the bar for the first time.

She glanced at them and then back at him, wordlessly.

He pursed his lips at her, taking the bag. "Thanks."

"Who is that woman?" she asked, craning her neck to see Cassidy who was out of view.

"She's a baker. She's the one I'm getting the cookies we talked about from."

"She doesn't look like any baker I've ever seen."

Jesse squinted out the front window in the direction Cassidy just walked. "It's not just me, right? She's like, sexy, isn't she?"

Kelly let her head drop to the side. "Oh, Jesse. You are not thinking about this, are you?"

"Thinking about what?"

"You just said you were doing business with her."

"So?"

"So you're going to fuck this up. You're gonna sleep with her and then we'll be down a cookie vendor."

"I'm not going to sleep with her," he said, grabbing the cups of sour beer and taking them to the bar.

Kelly followed behind him. "You will…if you can."

He stopped and jerked his head around. "What do you mean, if I can?"

"I mean that is a full-on woman. She's seasoned and sharp. She's got an air about her. She's low on bullshit tolerance, I can promise you that."

"You think I'm full of bullshit?"

"Oh, definitely."

Jesse knew he was full of bullshit. It was part of his bartender persona, the one that kept him protected and guarded. "That's hurtful."

Kelly followed him to the back door. "Don't do it, man."

He pointed at the bar. "That guy needs a refill."

When she turned around to see who he was pointing at, he slipped out the back door.

She was right. He had no business sleeping with Cassidy Anderson. Who was even to say she would have him? *How do you know what I'd do to you, Jesse?* His name coming off her puffy little lips was enough to make him sweat. That was a flirtation. She was flirting with him, right? Of course she was. He was Jesse Kirby. Girls flirted with him every day. Why should Cassidy Anderson be any different?

Because he cared what Cassidy Anderson thought of him. He wanted to know more about her. What did she do when she wasn't at the bakery? What did she eat? What did she read or watch? And more than anything, who did she date?

Chapter Three

Cassidy's cheeks were so hot she could bake those cookies she'd just dropped off on them. Why had she gone there with him? She'd sworn to herself that she wouldn't. She was going to drop off the cookies and leave. She had no intention of sitting down with him and talking business today, and she'd certainly not planned on shamelessly flirting the way she had.

How do you know what I'd do to you, Jesse? Jesus. She'd have been less obvious if she'd lifted her shirt and flashed him.

She parked behind Seaside Sweets and headed in through the back door, dropping off her purse in her desk drawer. She passed through the double swinging doors to find Marigold tapping away into her phone at the front counter. She looked up at Cassidy, a smile spreading across her lips. "Guess who just asked for your number?"

Cassidy gave her a look. "The pope?"

She poked Cassidy in the shoulder. "Jesse likes you."

"I just dropped the cookies off over there. He's probably got a business question."

"A chocolate chip emergency, for sure," Marigold said, tapping into her phone. Cassidy's phone dinged. "That's his contact. Set it up so you'll know who it is when he texts you."

Cassidy unlocked her phone and handed it to Marigold. "We made the deal. A buck fifty a cookie."

Marigold pecked into Cassidy's phone. "I'm guessing he'd have done that deal at any cost."

"How much weed have you been putting in the brownies around here? That young boy is not interested in my tired, old ass."

"Your ass is outstanding, for the record, and he is so interested in you. He asked Dane if you were seeing anyone and what your orientation was." Marigold handed Cassidy's phone back to her.

"My orientation? He thought I was gay?"

"Or pan, or bi, or questioning, or whatever. It's a legit question."

"What'd Dane tell him?"

"That to his knowledge, you were full-on straight." Marigold raised an eyebrow at her. "That was the correct answer, right?"

Cassidy rolled her eyes and checked the pans in the case to see what needed refilling.

"I don't know why I never thought to put the two of you together before. You're perfect for one another."

Cassidy huffed a laugh. "You've definitely been putting too much pot in the brownies."

"I'm serious. He's hot as blazes. Have you ever seen him with his shirt off?"

Cassidy held out both hands to her sides. "When would I have seen that? When did you see that?" she asked, getting a little jealous.

"Remember, I told you Dane's friend took us out on a boat a couple of weeks ago? That was him."

Cassidy imagined Jesse in a pair of low-slung board shorts that hung below his belly button, his tattooed chest on full display. She had no idea if he had tattoos on his chest. She just hoped.

"Just the three of you?" Cassidy asked, not sure what she was doing…gauging to see if he had a girlfriend, possibly? *Stop it, Cassidy.*

"He brought his friend Gracie."

"Ah." Figured.

"They really are just friends. They sort of bickered like brother and sister all day, in a cute way. Not obnoxious."

Cassidy combined a pan of muffins with a pan of cinnamon rolls. "That's wonderful. I'm going to start the cheese straws." Her phone dinged.

Marigold pointed at Cassidy's phone on the counter. "It's him, look!"

Cassidy glanced down at the phone, but it wasn't as if she could read it without her glasses. Just another reminder that she was middle-aged. Her twenty-twenty vision had gone AWOL.

The bell on the door dinged, and Marigold engaged with the customer. Cassidy headed back to the kitchen with the empty pan, once again thanking her lucky stars that Marigold had come to work with her. The customers loved her. She'd gotten to know the regulars and helped to create new regulars. But Cassidy suspected she only had a few more months of Marigold working there. She and Desiree had been putting together pop-up art shows that were taking off quite nicely. Cassidy suspected within the year, Marigold would be doing that full-time, so she knew to enjoy Marigold's company and stellar work ethic while it lasted.

Cassidy dropped the empty pan in the sink and then washed her hands, readying herself to start the cheese straws using puff pastry. She got it out of the refrigerator where it had been thawing, and was getting ready to go to work, but she hesitated, thinking about that message. He was a customer. There was nothing wrong with checking a text from a customer. She just wished this particular customer wasn't hot as blazes.

She went back out front and grabbed her phone off the counter, trying to avoid Marigold's knowing grin, but no such luck. Cassidy gave her a look as she headed back to the kitchen with her phone. She grabbed her pair of reading glasses from the top shelf above her workspace.

You forgot to tell me what you thought of the sour beer.

Cassidy dropped her phone onto the counter, staring at it like it had legs. *Just answer the stupid text*, she told herself.

She picked up the phone and thought hard, way too hard. She shook her head at herself and let out a deep breath, typing in the first thing she could think of.

Loved it.

She hit send and set the phone down. She stared at the dough in front of her for way too long. What had she been doing? The phone dinged again.

Your satisfaction is my number one priority.

Oh, Jesus Christ, she thought, but the smile on her face couldn't be stopped. She typed back.

You're my customer. Shouldn't I be the one saying that?

A moment passed, then the ellipsis popped up, giving her the tiniest little tingle in her belly. Ridiculous.

I tried one of your cookies. I'm satisfied.

What a relief. I can sleep tight tonight.

She bit her lip as she waited for his response.

That's good to know. Let me know if you ever have trouble sleeping. I can help out with that.

The double doors swung open. "So?" Marigold asked, her big eyes wide open. Cassidy fumbled with her phone and dropped it onto the floor. They both bent down at the same time to pick it up, Marigold staring at her neck. "Oh, my gosh. Look at you. You are totally blushing."

Cassidy pocketed her phone and walked over to the sink to wash her hands again. "I'm not."

"What did that text say?"

"Nothing. He just wanted to know if I liked this new beer he had me try out when I dropped off the cookies."

"You had a beer with him?"

"Like two sips. We talked business the whole time." Cassidy headed back over to the dough and got out her cutter.

"He is smoking hot. You should totally go there."

"No way," Cassidy said, setting down the knife. There was another step in this process. She just couldn't think of it for the life of her.

"Why not?"

"Because I've got to do business with this man. I'm not sleeping with him. Besides, he's like twenty."

"He's twenty-nine, for the record."

Cassidy laughed out loud at this. After a second good look at him, she'd exaggerated his age in her imagination from twenty-five to early thirties, only to justify her own attraction to him. Knowing now he was still in his twenties, she felt silly.

Marigold put her hands on her hips. "What is so freaking funny?"

"He's a child, Marigold."

"He's like my age."

"Exactly. You're like a niece to me."

"That man is not your nephew. He's a super-hot, young guy who's interested. Let him take you out."

"It's not like he's asking." Her phone dinged on cue.

"Check it!" Marigold pointed at Cassidy's pocket like it was on fire.

Cassidy let her head drop to the side. "Will you please chill out?"

"Not until you read that message." She held up both hands and headed out front. "I won't even look over your shoulder."

The bell on the front door dinged, and Marigold greeted the customer, leaving Cassidy alone with her phone. She pulled it out of her pocket and was really irritated at the letdown she felt when it was Maya's name across the screen and not Jesse's. On any other day, seeing Maya's name on her phone would have lifted her up.

Party time! Please join Bo and me Saturday night for a barbecue, weather permitting. If it doesn't cooperate, we'll head inside for a cozy but fun time anyway! See you at five. Bring nothing but your lovely selves.

Cassidy heaved a sigh and headed back to her dough, trying to decide what dessert she would bring. But as she sprinkled cheese and twisted dough, all she could think about was the tattooed man across town at his bar, offering to wear her out until she was sated and sleepy…at least that was what she dreamed he was implying.

Chapter Four

The doorbell rang and Cassidy called, "Coming!" She hadn't left enough time to do much with her wild and wavy hair, but unless she pulled it straight there wasn't much to be done there. Besides, it was just her regular crew tonight at Bo and Maya's house. They all liked her despite her out-of-control hair, thank goodness.

She flipped off light switches and headed that way, grabbing her small purse on the way out. "Long time no see," she said to Marigold, who she'd just left at the shop an hour ago.

"Sick of me yet?" Marigold asked.

Cassidy gave her a smile. "Never."

As they approached the SUV, Cassidy waved at Dane who was in the driver's seat. "Dane's gonna be DD tonight, bless him," Marigold said.

"Good guy you've got there."

"Oh," Marigold said. "We're picking up Shayla

and Chase in Seagrove, so would you mind scooting to the way way back when you get in?"

"Of course not."

Cassidy opened the door and stilled. Jesse sat in the third row with a sideways grin on his face, giving her stomach a little flip.

"I don't bite…unless requested," he said.

She tried futilely to cool her heated cheeks as she climbed through the seats and swung her behind past him to get settled in beside him. "I didn't see your name on the group text invite."

He lifted an eyebrow. "You were looking for it?"

Cassidy buckled in for the ride. "I was just checking the guest list. Not for anyone in particular."

"Everyone settled?" Marigold asked.

"All set," Jesse said.

Marigold cut a quick glance at Cassidy with a grin. Cassidy would strangle her for this later.

"I saw Bo at his shop on Thursday," Jesse said. "He sold me a paddleboard and invited me to come tonight."

"How hospitable of him. How's the board?"

"Haven't been out yet. Waiting on Mother Nature to bring the heat."

She nodded and checked her purse to make sure she'd brought her phone. Not that she needed it for anything. "How are the cookies selling?"

"You'd know if you delivered them in person. I haven't seen you all week."

As much as Cassidy had wanted to see him, she had avoided his bar like the plague. That last text he'd sent was too tempting, and she had been getting too close to taking him up on his offer. She'd texted him the next day letting him know in a purely professional tone not to stop by for the cookies, and that Seaside Sweets would deliver them daily. "Something wrong with Marigold's delivery services?"

"She's fantastic, but she's taken."

"And your delivery person needs to be single?"

"I don't know. Would that qualify you?"

She looked out the window, tamping down her smile, or trying to.

His phone dinged, and he read a text and then typed back. The exchange went on for a few minutes, keeping her guessing. He put the phone face down on his knee and glanced over at her.

She pulled her hair back out of her face and stared out the window at the passing condos and restaurants of 30A.

"You didn't answer my question," he said.

"You got busy." She indicated the phone on his knee.

"Work."

"Ah," she said, raising her eyebrow.

"I'm serious. It was work."

"Okay," she said.

He poked her in the leg. "Jealous?"

Despite the frenzy in her stomach from his touch, she slid him a look, and then put her attention back on the road.

"I'm a hundred percent single, if anyone's curious," he said.

"How wonderful for you."

"And you?" he asked.

She let out a sigh and kept her eyes on the road.

"Tell me your story. Have you ever been married?"

She gave him her attention. "No."

Both of his eyebrows went up. "Really?"

She shrugged. "Yeah. What's so shocking about that?"

He offered a hand toward her. "It's just hard to believe some guy didn't snatch you up."

"Well, I'm not a television at Walmart on Black Friday."

He smiled and then looked out his window. They pulled down Chase and Shayla's wooded street and then into their driveway. "Nice house," Jesse said.

"You should see the pool and outdoor kitchen in the back. Where do you live?" Cassidy asked, curiosity getting the better of her.

His cheeks turned pink. "Above my bar," he said, his voice losing its confidence and bravado. "I bought the whole space."

"Wow," she said. "That's all yours? The bar and the space above it?" She may have been overdoing it a little, but he seemed like he could use the ego boost. Chase's house was impressive, but Chase was also a millionaire many times over.

Jesse cut his eyes at her. "You can stop pretending to be impressed any time now."

"I wasn't—"

The door opened and Chase's voice boomed into the small space. "Hey friends. Who's ready for some barbecue?"

Shayla slapped his butt which was up in her face as he climbed over to the seat on the far side. "We're not having actual barbecue. We're grilling."

"If it's meat I'm eating it." He held out his big hand to Jesse. "Chase O'Neil. I know you, don't I?"

"The Bohemian Guppy. Jesse Kirby."

"Of course. You were out of context for a second, but I'm tracking now." He glanced between Cassidy and him, and she realized he was thinking they were on a date. She sunk down in her seat a little.

Jesse glanced at her, and then back at Chase. "I bought a paddleboard from Bo a couple of days ago and he invited me. Dane was kind enough to give me a ride."

"Ah," Chase said, seeming only partially satisfied with the answer.

Chase turned around to say something to Dane and Marigold, and Cassidy slid Jesse a small smile. Jesse gave her a little shrug and then checked his phone.

Shayla peered over the seat. "Hey girl."

Cassidy took Shayla's hand and squeezed it. "Hey yourself."

Shayla turned to Jesse. "I'm Shayla. I'm Bo's sister." She held out her hand to him.

He shook it. "I see the resemblance."

"I won't hold that comment against you," Shayla said with a cute smile, and then gave her attention to Chase, who started a story that blessedly went on for miles. Cassidy got lost in the trees flashing by her on Highway 98 as Jesse flipped through his phone.

Jesse watched Cassidy from across the room, engaged in conversation with Maya, who was Bo's wife. She hadn't been left alone a moment the whole night. When someone was lucky enough to engage

35

her in a one-on-one, they always looked a little disappointed when someone else came up. He'd come to Bo's party understanding that he wouldn't know many people, and also knowing it'd be mostly couples. He was willing to make that sacrifice for a shot at getting to know Cassidy better, but he couldn't get near her.

The guys of the group had been beyond kind, engaging him in conversation, asking about his bar and everything else they could think of, making a true effort to include him in this group of clearly tight-knit friends. But Jesse couldn't keep his mind or his eyes off Cassidy.

Jesse stood near the sliding glass door, pretending to admire a grouping of photographic art, signed by Ashe Bianchi, who Jesse knew to be dating Dane's twin brother Ethan. There were so many layers to this friend group his buddy Dane was becoming a part of. Shayla joined the conversation with Cassidy and her friends, and Cassidy finally met Jesse's glance for the first time all night. He held it, not willing to let her off the hook. She gave him the smallest hint of a smile that boosted his mood tremendously. A moment later, she met his gaze again, pumping his confidence enough for him to make his move. He nodded toward the sliding glass door, and then went outside, hoping like hell she'd follow him. As the sliding glass door opened, he held his breath until he saw her slide through and glance around the yard.

"Hey," he said, his voice coming out lower than he intended.

She turned to meet his gaze, and then slid the door closed and stepped over to where he was standing.

"How are you holding up?" she asked. "They were grilling you pretty hard earlier."

"I'm all good. They're nice guys."

She nodded. "That they are."

"You're popular with this group. They all can't seem to get enough of you."

She waved him off. "I'm the new toy. I've been gone a couple of months. They'll get sick of me soon."

"Do you ever take a compliment?" he asked.

"Sure, if you want to tell me you like my shirt or my hair."

He took a chance and touched her hair, playing with it a little. "I like your hair."

Her cheeks went pink as she tugged at a strand. "It's sort of got a life of its own."

He let go of the strand he was messing with, and she brushed her hair back out of her face, but it just sprung right back into place. God, he could kiss her right now, but he knew better.

She glanced around the backyard. "I know we're just getting air, but it feels like we're doing something sinister out here."

Oh, the ways he could respond to that. "Maybe it's the stormy sky." They both looked up at it, the dark clouds moving in opposite directions, stirring up trouble.

She met his gaze. "I don't know if I can put the blame on it."

"You think I'm the one making it menacing out here?"

She smiled at him, heating up his body temperature despite the cool breeze. "You're

37

definitely trouble."

"I wouldn't mind being in trouble with you."

She grinned, looking down at the ground, and he mentally gave himself a point, hoping he could keep walking this tightrope without falling on his ass.

"How about it, Cassidy? Wanna get into some trouble with me tonight?"

She narrowed her gaze making his heart speed up. "One of these days I'm going to take you up on your offers…see if you'll actually follow through on them."

It was all he could do to keep from kissing her, but he had to hold back. "Don't tease me."

The sliding glass door opened and Maya peeked out. "Oh, I'm sorry. I didn't mean to interrupt."

"No, you're not interrupting," Cassidy said. "We were just getting some air."

"Oh, okay. I was going to serve your pies. Is that okay?"

"Of course it's okay. I'll be right there."

Maya went back inside, and Cassidy turned to him with a guilty grin. She pinched at his waist, causing a bolt through his stomach. He tried to reduce his grin as he followed her inside. As she headed to the kitchen, Bo called him over to where he was standing with Blake in the living room watching a game on a humungous television.

"You doing okay?" Bo asked. "Can I get you anything?"

Jesse had to give these people a five-star rating for hospitality and inclusivity. "No, I think I'm good."

"I don't guess you've had a chance to try your board yet, huh?"

"Not yet, but as soon as Mother Nature heats us up, I'll be out there. I think we're supposed to have a pretty day tomorrow."

"Yep," Bo said, Blake nodding along. Bo sort of eyed Jesse. "I saw you come in from outside with Cassidy. Are the two of you here together?"

Blake glared at him. "Not that it's any of our business."

"No, we're not together," Jesse said. "We both did ride here with Dane and Marigold though."

"That's right," Blake said. "You're a good buddy of Dane's aren't you?"

"Yeah, we went to college together."

"Must be nice having someone here from home," Blake said.

"It is," Jesse said, glancing into the kitchen. As hard as he tried, he couldn't keep his eyes off of Cassidy, even when she was cutting pies.

Bo glanced in that same direction and then back to Jesse, his gaze narrowing at him. "You sure nothing's going on between the two of you?"

"Bo," Blake barked.

Bo held up the hand that wasn't holding a beer bottle. "What? I'm curious."

"Are you her ex?" Jesse asked.

Bo lifted his chin in challenge, wordlessly.

"Fuck no, he's not," Blake said.

Bo's eyes went wide at Blake. "Will you shut the hell up for once?"

Jesse couldn't help a smile at these two guys who seemed more like brothers than friends, though they didn't look anything alike.

"Bo," Maya called from the kitchen, "would you

please help me with the ice cream?"

"Sure thing, darlin'," Bo said, hopping to his wife's command, leaving Jesse alone with Blake.

"How do you know Bo?" Jesse asked.

"I met him through Chase a few years back."

"Oh, I just assumed you two had known each other since you were kids or something. You act kind of like brothers."

Blake glanced at Bo in the kitchen with a smile. "Bo's the closest thing I've ever had to a brother." He turned back to Jesse. "He acts like a horse's ass sometimes, but he'd give you the shirt off his back if he thought you needed it."

Jesse nodded, feeling envious of their close relationship. He and his own brother were once that close, but they damn sure weren't anymore. "Sometimes we pick our family."

Blake's eyebrows went up in consideration as he glanced around the room. "Or they pick you."

"Mmm," Jesse uttered, taking a swig of beer. He didn't let people get close to him, not since college. Dane was the nearest thing to a best friend Jesse had, but Jesse was even careful to let Dane in. When people got too close, that gave them the ability to hurt you. Jesse wouldn't ever let that happen again.

"So you're not married, I'm assuming," Blake said.

"No, not my thing."

"It wasn't my thing either, until I met Seanna." Blake looked over at an attractive, curvy girl who was talking with Dane and Marigold. The contented adoration in his gaze almost made Jesse envious. Blake turned back toward him. "You're not seeing anyone seriously?" He held up a hand. "I'm not trying to be nosey. Just making conversation."

Jesse was starting to wonder if Blake and Bo had a good cop/bad cop routine going on. "No. I don't really see anyone seriously. That's also not my thing."

Blake nodded as if this made perfect sense and turned his attention to the game, but his brow was furrowed like he was deep in thought. After a moment of standing there watching a game Jesse couldn't care less about and Blake seemed uninterested in, Blake said, "Don't rule it out. Excuse me." He headed down the hallway toward the bathroom, leaving Jesse a little dazed.

Cassidy stared out the window into the dark night as they headed back down 30A toward their homes, the car decidedly quieter than it had been on their way to the party. Bellies were full of food and drink, and everyone was sated. In the front, Marigold and Dane held hands, their elbows sitting side by side on the shared armrest. In the middle Chase and Shayla were in quiet conversation, smiling at one another as Chase reached over and rubbed on her leg, Shayla covering his hand with her own, squeezing tightly.

Cassidy had been single most of her adult life. Somewhere along the way, dating had turned into a chore. Getting to know someone and sticking with them despite all their faults and her own had become a task she couldn't master. She was picky, not when it came to looks though. She'd dated men who were twice her weight, bald-headed, and just flat-out unattractive. The outside had never mattered much to her. She was always digging deeper to find a heart that complimented her own. There'd been times she found a shallow heart, then there'd been times she'd found a man's heart was bigger and more giving than her own, and she'd not felt worthy of their love. Whatever her process had been, it'd failed to bring her a happily ever after.

She'd never thought she needed that until she watched these friends of hers coupling up around her, the smiles on their faces so wide she thought they all might burst from love to give. She'd never thought she'd say or even think it, but for the first time, she wondered if she'd made the wrong choice somewhere along the way.

She felt a poke in her leg and turned to find Jesse giving her that look that he must have given a thousand women in his time…that look that drew women to him like a bee to a hive, and here she was, falling in line just like the others. She was certainly no stronger than they were.

She rested her head against the back of the seat, staring at him with a hint of a smile.

"You looked deep in thought just then," he said.

She gave a small shrug. "Nothing earth-shattering."

"I imagine your thoughts would interest me."

Her smile grew. "You give me way too much credit."

"I doubt that."

He reached over and ran a finger across her knuckles, waking up her sleepy body. She was either too tired or too interested to resist. He landed on her ring finger. "I can't believe you've never been married. It seems like everyone gets married."

"You're not married," she said.

"Not my thing."

She huffed a laugh. "Clearly, it's not mine either."

He narrowed his gaze at her. "I'll bet you've been asked."

She shrugged her response.

"Probably more than once," he said, gauging her.

"What about you?" she asked, eager to divert the attention from herself. "Have you ever done the asking?"

His brow furrowed, and he seemed to lose some of his confidence as he glanced out the window, mouth open, but words not yet coming out. She'd found his Achilles heel.

She waved herself off. "Doesn't matter. The past is where it should be."

They pulled into Chase and Shayla's driveway and said their goodbyes with promises to get together again soon. But Cassidy wondered where her place was in this group. Despite her age, she'd always felt a part of the group because they were all single like her. But as they continued to couple up, and knowing it was just a matter of time before they all started having children, she wondered how much longer she would feel comfortable being a part of them.

"Are you okay?" Jesse asked.

She blinked herself awake. "Oh, yeah. Just tired."

"Do you maybe have one more drink in you?" he asked as they turned onto 30A.

"At your bar?" she asked with a grin.

"I'm always up for a drink at my bar, but we could get one close to your house. I could walk you home afterward."

She gave him a look.

"I'm serious. I just want a minute to hang with you. You were so popular tonight, I didn't even have the opportunity to really talk to you."

As they plowed through Seagrove headed toward Seaside, her mind raced, weighing her options. The idea of spending an hour at a bar with him was definitely tempting. The idea of bringing him back to her bed was downright mouthwatering. But the logical part of her brain told her she was feeling vulnerable and this was a trap she'd regret falling into tomorrow.

She'd had one-night-stands in her time, but none of them had left her feeling great the next day. She applauded these young women who owned their sexuality and had no qualms about sleeping around on their terms. But Cassidy came from a time where free love came with a stigma. Sure, times had changed, thank God, but Cassidy hadn't necessarily changed with them. To her, sex had always been something she'd waited for. She liked knowing that her partner cared about her and probably would want to call her afterward. The handful of times she'd given herself to a man and he'd not called her back had crushed her and left her feeling vulnerable and used. She liked to be in control of her emotions.

She gazed into Jesse's blue eyes, and then moved down to his strong, tattooed arms, his right hand housing two silver rings. This young man was certified hot as fuck. There was no arguing it. And he was seducing her tired, forty-four-year-old ass. What was she waiting for?

As they passed Seaside Sweets, Cassidy's street was just around the corner. Dane put on the turn signal, and Cassidy's heartbeat ratcheted up, because she knew she was getting ready to do something completely out of character, damn the consequences.

"I've got a bottle of wine at my house," she said. "Wanna have a drink on the beach?"

Chapter Five

Cassidy had grabbed two quilts, one for them to lay on the beach and another to cover up with. Sure, she understood she was out of her mind, taking a young guy to the beach when it was probably forty-five degrees out there, but this was the safe way. If they opened that bottle of wine in her living room, she would be toast. If they had this drink on the beach, covered in jackets and blankets, all would be safe. That was the theory.

After they got the first blanket spread onto the dark beach, she handed him a hoodie. "I'll be honest, I don't know where this came from. It's been at the house for a couple of years, but it's clean. I wear it when I want to be swallowed whole," she said, babbling out of nervousness.

"Thanks," he said, and then pulled the hoodie over his head.

"Is it too cold out here?" she asked.

"Not for me. Are you okay?"

"Yeah." She held up the other blanket she was holding. I brought this one to lay over our laps."

He smiled. "That's perfect."

She sat on the blanket, rolling her eyes at herself. What the hell was she doing there?

He pulled the wine bottle out of the bag they'd brought, and poured her a generous portion into a plastic cup.

"Thanks," she said, taking it from him.

He poured his own and then sat down beside her, pulling the blanket she'd laid out over his lap. "I love the ocean at night like this."

"Mmm," she muttered. "I haven't been down here at night in years."

He glanced over at her. "Tell me about Jamaica."

"What do you want to know?"

"What work do you do there?"

"It depends on the project. This time we were building houses. Have you been over there?"

"Does that nude resort everyone goes to count?" he asked. She gave him a look, and he smiled. "I'm kidding. No, I haven't been, but I've heard the stories."

"This is a different part of Jamaica," she said.

"I understand that. Tell me about it."

"It's not much. It's not enough, for sure. But we do what we can with the time and resources we have. Todd, who runs the project, does the fundraising through the year, and then when he gathers the resources, he puts together a team."

"Do you go every year?" he asked.

"Not every year. I've been several years, but it

47

doesn't always work out. Sometimes it's summertime when he gets the project ready, and I can't be gone from the shop then. The stars happened to align this go-around."

"So you've been working with these people for a while?"

"For about twenty years, I guess. We did our first job when we were…" She caught herself, realizing she was getting ready to give him a definite age for her. She had never once been ashamed of her age, but sitting here on this beach with this guy her body bowed to for some reason, she wasn't prepared to give that information just yet. "In our twenties," she finished.

He studied her. "I've never done anything like that. It must make you feel good."

"More than that it makes me feel helpless. Todd's an amazing guy and he does so much. I do a tiny little bit then come back here and bake brownies. It makes me feel silly." She'd never put that into words before, but as it came out she realized how true it was.

"Two months of work is amazing."

"Not at all. Todd has devoted his whole life to this stuff. I do it for a finite time, knowing I'm coming back to my beach home and bakery in Seaside. Honestly, I just feel inadequate sometimes."

He shook his head. "What should that make me feel?"

She touched his arm. "I'm so sorry. I wasn't trying to make you feel guilty."

"No, I should. I'm caught up in my own world. Sometimes it feels like my bar is my whole identity."

She nodded. "When I've spent a week straight at

the bakery, I can start to feel that, too. These are our jobs. We shouldn't let our jobs define us, even if we do own the businesses."

He met her gaze, his expression serious. "For sure."

"Tell me about paddleboarding," she said.

He waved her off with an embarrassed look on his face.

"No, I'm serious. That's really interesting to me."

He reached up and scratched the back of his head. "I don't know. It's just something I do. I love the water. Jet skis, paddleboards, parasailing…"

"Oh my God," she said, putting her hand over her heart. "I can't even."

"Are you serious?"

"Oh yeah. I'm terrified of the water. I'm more than happy to sit here and look at it, but the idea of being out there flying above it makes me nauseous."

"I could take you out. Help you get over your fear."

"No thanks."

He nudged her. "Let me."

She searched his gaze, refusing to fall for his charm. "What's your game, Jesse?"

He blinked. "What do you mean?"

"Do you get off on boosting an old lady's ego?"

He turned his body so he was facing her full-on. "I don't know what the fuck old lady you're talking about."

She rolled her eyes at him, gathering her knees to her chest, and then pulling the blanket over them.

"What's *your* game?" he asked.

"Me?" Her eyes went wide.

"You could tell me to fuck off at any time, but you don't seem to mind being with me."

She sat there looking at him, speechless, heat seeping up through her neck. Though she could feel her emotions taking over her sense of logic and reason, she was powerless to control them. She didn't get embarrassed often, but when she did that was *her* Achilles heel.

"How about this? Fuck off."

"I would if I thought you were serious."

She narrowed her gaze at him, pointing between the two of them. "This works on women? This full-of-yourself, cocky, arrogant swagger?"

"I don't know. Does it?"

She blinked, not knowing what the hell to do with this beautiful creature who she wanted to strangle and screw all at the same time.

He set his cup down in the sand and then faced her. "I'll tell you this right now, flirtations and games aside, I'm fucking losing my mind I want you so bad. Ever since the night Marigold introduced me to you at my bar a couple of weeks ago, I've done nothing but dream of what your body tastes like, from your mouth all the way down."

Cassidy's core heated like a blow torch.

He came closer. "So before you tell me to fuck off, you better decide if that's what you really want. Because what I want is my body on top of yours."

Her mouth met his, and she took in his delicious lips with a hunger so ravenous she thought she might swallow him up. He tasted like sweet wine and nineteen-ninety-six. His hand snaked around to the back of her neck, his fingers threading through her hair. The older she had gotten the less interested in French kisses she had become, because the men she'd been with had always been sweet but nothing to write home about in bed. But she could live decades with this man's tongue wrapped around hers.

Before she knew it, she was horizontal, and he had his wish, his body on top of hers. She assumed he was bullshitting her with his declaration of how he wanted her, but at this point she didn't even care. She wrapped her legs around his back as he settled in on top of her, still kissing her mouth. What had happened to her wine cup? Finally, he pulled away, his breath as heavy as hers. He smoothed her hair out of her face, staring into her eyes. "Fuck," was all he said, and then he went back in for more kissing.

She threaded her fingers through his hair as he continued to kiss her, wondering how she was going to live without his tongue in her mouth when this was over, remembering the beauty of the perfectly executed French kiss. Damn, it'd been a long time.

As he moved on top of her, she practically gasped as his hard cock pressed against her center. Oh God, the wonder of the young guy's naturally achieved erection. Her hand reached for it out of pure need. A young, hard cock, ready for her. Nobody else was around in this dark Seaside night. She ran her hand over it though his jeans, but that simply would not do. She undid his pants and her hand gripped his cock which was free of any form of underwear.

She closed her eyes as he pulled off of her, giving her space between them, but continued to kiss her neck. As she gripped this rock-hard cock, all she could think about was how rare it was these days. Just last month, that second time she was with Todd, his loose erection had lost steam halfway through their lovemaking, and he'd fallen off of her, defeated and ashamed. She'd spent the next three days trying to subtly boost his ego to make up for it. But now, here was this cock that was as strong and solid as a flagpole.

"Fuck, Cassidy," he breathed into her neck as she felt a little drip on her thumb. She didn't realize her appreciation and playing around with him was having a real effect. Jesus, it took a fifteen-minute blow job to get the old guys she'd been with recently ready to roll.

He pulled away and met her gaze. "I've got condoms."

Oh fuck. That was where they were headed, wasn't it? What else did she think was happening here? She wasn't thinking. She was reveling.

Was she actually going to let this man enter her? She'd been sworn off one-nighters for so long, but here she was, poised for one. If she did this with him, how was she going to do business with him with a straight face? Goodness gracious, she was holding his dick in her hand. She was pretty sure she'd passed the point of return.

"Can you double-up?" she asked. Cassidy came up in the '80s and '90s when AIDS was a death sentence. She understood people his age were likely less concerned about condom usage, which was what troubled her even more. Even though it could be manageable thanks to advancements in medicine, she still didn't want it or anything else that was spread through unprotected sex.

"Yeah, I've got two."

Of course he did. He probably had ten.

As he sat up, kicking off his jeans, she slid out of hers, the cold air hitting her legs like a slap in the face. He slid the first condom on and then the second like a master. He pulled the blanket over his back, and then lowered himself down to her. He kissed her again, but this time slow and sensual, the tip of his cock teasing her clit. God, she was so wound up she thought she might blast off.

He pushed inside of her and she gripped his shoulders as his pure, unadulterated breadth consumed her. Although it was a brisk, spring evening, the heat under that blanket must have been a thousand degrees. He slowed down, pumping into her with intentional, deliberate movements. He kissed her again and she rocked her hips up to meet his thrusts. She gripped his shoulder blades as the buildup inside of her started its ascent.

"Will you come with me?" he whispered into her ear.

"Yes," she breathed back. God, could she? It'd been ages since she had through intercourse. These days it was all about getting the man through the task. But this man needed no assistance.

He pumped harder and faster, starting a pounding rhythm for the both of them to sail away to. As the intensity inside of her got to be more than she could handle, she let out breathy moans, signaling him that it was happening for her so he could go along with her.

"Oh, fuck," he said as he collapsed onto her,

breathing into the crook of her neck. She could barely catch her own breath as their chests rose and fell together in unison through their suffocating sweatshirts. He rolled off of her and lay on his back, staring at the stars.

The reality of what had just happened started to seep in like a fluorescent office light. What was she doing? This was the beach in front of her home. Sure, her neighbors with beach views had likely not been able to see them in the pitch black dark this far away, but still. She reached under the blanket for her jeans.

"What's your hurry?" he asked, running his hand down her thigh. Damn, his touch. Give her five minutes and she'd be ready to go again. But she had to go home and process what she'd just done.

"I need to get home."

He searched her gaze, but she didn't give anything up. "You don't want to sleep under the stars with me?"

She could. She would roll over and settle into the crook of his arm, snuggled under the quilt until dawn broke. She could watch the sun come up with him.

It was time to wake up out of her alternate reality. This man had worked his magic on her and she'd fallen for it. She didn't blame him. She played the game as hard as he did. But now she had to accept that he would move on to the next girl, one fifteen or twenty years younger than her. She couldn't or wouldn't compete with that. And if he was in her life at all, she'd be wanting to do what they just did over and over and in a million different ways and formats. Best to cut ties now before she was even deeper in.

She smiled. "That sounds nice. But I want to sleep

in my bed."

He nodded, gauging her. "Okay." Was that a flash of hurt in his eyes? She really couldn't tell.

They both slid into their jeans and then stood, Cassidy folding up the top blanket and Jesse gathering the plastic cups, and hopefully the condom.

"Did you get the…"

He held up the plastic cups. "Yep. In here."

She nodded, and picked up the bottom blanket to shake it out. He helped, getting the other corners. Once they'd shaken it a bit, they walked toward each other, and he handed her his side. He picked up the other side of the blanket, and then walked toward her to hand her that side, but instead of walking away that time, he cupped both hands over hers, which were still gripping the blanket. "I had a really fun time tonight, and not just here."

She swallowed, nodding her head. "Yeah, definitely. Our friends are really great."

He just stared at her, wordlessly calling her out on her bullshit. She backed away, continuing to fold the blanket. He loaded up with everything else, and they headed up the beach in silence. As they approached her house, she remembered he didn't have a car. "Oh, I can drive you home."

He pulled out his phone. "I already ordered an Urban Ride, down on the beach."

She nodded, and he followed her to the house where he set the stuff down on her dining room table. He jerked a thumb toward the door. "I'll see you, okay?" he asked.

"I'm sure we will," she said.

Lights flooded the street in front of her house, and

he held up a hand in a wave as he backed out the doorway. She collapsed onto the couch, pulling her hair out of her face. This was not her finest hour. Not only was she ashamed of giving in to temptation, but she'd exited that situation with less grace than a grizzly bear at a tea party. She could have slept there on the beach with him. She would have loved that, actually. But she didn't like the feelings she was forming for him. She would not confuse lust for real feelings. She was smarter and more experienced than that.

Her phone dinged from somewhere. She peered around for her purse and found it in the kitchen. A message from Jesse, perhaps? This would be her opportunity to make things…not right, but better. An apology of some sort for rushing him out? She wasn't sure that felt right. She knew she owed one, she just didn't know how to deliver it.

She located her phone and was disappointed to find it was just a notification that someone had followed the shop on Instagram. But underneath it was a text notification…from Todd.

Hey, really missing you here in Jamaica. I don't mean romantically. Well, we both know that's a lie, but seriously, I do miss you. I'm working on a new project. Hoping to have the funds ready to go by October 1. I know you're busy, but I really hope you can make it for at least a while.

She closed her eyes. Like she needed something else to make her feel like shit tonight.

Chapter Six

Jesse paddled out into the ocean, the low tide making his job easier than usual. He'd come out there to get his mind off things and just focus on the water, but even the peace of the ocean couldn't save his thoughts today.

If he'd ever had a woman kiss him like that before, he damn sure didn't remember it. She kissed him like every moment their mouths were connected meant something. God he was starting to sound like an idiot, but he couldn't help it. The way she slid her fingers into his hair and wrapped her legs behind his back, rocking her hips up to meet his…damn. And then when she wrapped her hand around his cock, fuck, he almost lost it. The way she stroked him, slowly sliding her hand up and down like she wanted to memorize every muscle made him desperate to be inside her. The whole thing went by entirely too fast, mostly because of him rushing it. He couldn't help it though. He wanted her way too damn much.

The worst mistake he'd made was rolling off of her. As soon as he did that, she left him and went to another place, one where he didn't belong. She was done with him then. All he could think about was the many times he'd had sex with some girl from the bar, and then the moment he was done, he wanted away. That was how she'd felt about him.

It'd been four days since he'd seen her, and his feelings only seemed to grow stronger every day. He couldn't figure out why he couldn't let her go. Every moment he was around her he became more interested in her, and when he was away, he just spent his time wondering about her. He wanted to know more about her work in Jamaica, but she hadn't seemed to want to talk much about it, except for the several times she mentioned how wonderful *Todd* was. A hundred bucks said this Todd guy had a thing for her, and probably vice versa.

He paddled back in. It was too damned cold out there. It'd gotten up above seventy, but the water was a different story. After he washed up on the beach, he hauled his board up on his shoulder and headed back toward the bar. Two girls sat in beach chairs smiling at him.

He smiled back. Now, all he had to do was stop and drum up a conversation like he'd done a million times. But his feet just kept going right by them.

Cassidy's heartbeat increased as she walked the streets of Grayton toward Jesse's bar. The beach access lot she normally used was full, and so was every spot for a good square mile thanks to the gorgeous day. March was all over the place weather-wise in South Walton, so people came out in droves on the days they could.

She'd chickened out and sent Marigold with the cookie order on Tuesday. She just couldn't bring herself to come. Of course, Marigold had asked a million questions. Cassidy supposed she'd had a right to since Jesse had gotten out at Cassidy's house on Saturday night. Cassidy had been vague, but Marigold was no fool.

Cassidy took a deep breath as she opened the door to Jesse's bar. A couple of servers hustled around, but Cassidy didn't spot Jesse anywhere. One of the young women approached Cassidy and pointed at her. "Seaside Sweets, right?"

"Yes." Cassidy proffered the container, and the girl took it.

"Where's Marigold today?"

"Um, she's holding down the fort at the bakery."

"Ah," the girl said, taking the box from her. "Well thanks."

Cassidy hung around a second, and the girl furrowed her brow. "Do we owe you a check? I can grab some cash out of the register if you have an invoice."

"No. Actually...is Jesse around?"

"No, I don't think so." She glanced around. "Anyone know where Jesse is?" she shouted through the bar.

A blond girl filling a napkin dispenser said, "He's at the beach."

"Crap. Sorry," the woman said to Cassidy. "Do you want me to have him call you when he gets back?"

The door opened and in came a paddleboard first, and then a shirtless, barefooted man with a tattoo on his shoulder. She swallowed hard.

He heaved the board upright and set it down, and then met her gaze with clear surprise in his expression. "Hey."

Cassidy pointed at the server, still holding the cookie box. "I made the cookie delivery."

"Cool. Thanks. Do you have my invoice yet?"

"No, I meant to bring it. I'll have it ready with tomorrow's delivery."

The server pointed at Jesse. "Tell her about my idea with the menu."

He ran his hand through his wet hair as Cassidy tried to look at his face and nowhere else. "Kelly wanted to see if you'd be okay if we added your logo to the cookie item on the menu," he said.

"People love supporting local," Kelly said. "It's as much about sales for us as it is promotion for you. Can you send us a logo?"

"Sure. I'll have my designer do that."

"Cool," Kelly said and was off to the kitchen, leaving Cassidy alone with Jesse.

Cassidy glanced around. "Um, can we talk somewhere for just a quick second?"

"Sure," he said, picking up his board. He led her to a door that said, EMERGENCY EXIT ONLY. ALARM WILL SOUND, and pushed it open, no alarm sounding. He maneuvered his board through the doorway and then rested his sweet ass against the door, letting her walk through to what turned out to be a stairwell. He hefted his board expertly up onto a wall mount, the muscles in his tattooed arms rippling as he worked. He turned back around and faced her, his shorts sagging, those muscles below the stomach that form a broken V on broad display.

She glanced around at another door that must have exited to the outside, and then to the staircase in front of her. She pointed upward. "So, is this your apartment?"

"Yeah, did you want to…"

"No, no. I just," she said, inhaling a deep breath, "I just came here to say that I'm sorry about the other night."

He frowned.

"I think you probably realize that I sort of freaked out a bit after we…" She trailed off, unable to believe that she somehow had lost part of her own vocabulary.

"Had sex?" Jesse asked.

She closed her eyes, the heat seeping up to her ears. "Yes, thank you." This was ridiculous. He had moved on from her now, was probably onto the next girl already. For all she knew, he'd already slept with some other girl. He was a bartender with an apartment above his bar. How convenient did it get?

She just had to spit this nonsense out so she could move on and never see him again. She'd send Marigold with the cookie order from now on, and if she couldn't come, Cassidy would hire a courier, or just admit that cookie recipes can be found on the backs of chocolate chip bags.

She met his gaze, trying to garner her courage. "Jesse, what happened the other night…I don't do that."

"Okay," he said, resting his hands on his hips, his six-pack on full display.

Look up, Cassidy. Look up.

"I realize that it's no big deal and that people have one-night-stands all the time. But I come from a time where that wasn't as prevalent as it is now, and I've never really enjoyed them like many women do."

He lowered his chin. "You didn't enjoy yourself?"

She held up both hands. "No, I very much enjoyed myself. I'm just trying to explain why I had such an…" He inched toward her, causing her to lose track of what she'd been saying. "Ungraceful exit," she somehow managed to finish saying. Despite her pleas with herself, she looked down at his stomach. "Is that a raven tattoo?"

He touched it with both sets of his fingertips. "Yeah, I'm sort of a book nerd. I love Poe."

Her exhale of the breath she'd been holding was loud and included a little chuckle, because this was just getting ridiculous. A book nerd? Was he kidding her?

Her gaze slid to the other side which showcased a tattoo of a self-effacing quote about masculinity. She studied it, her brain reaching for its place but coming up short. She met his gaze, making a question with her eyebrows.

"Hemingway," he said. "*The Old Man and the Sea.*"

Geez. The fact that he loved books enough to plaster tattoos celebrating them on his body just made her even more fascinated with him. *Stop it, Cassidy.*

She shook her head, trying to clear her brain for

the task ahead. "So anyway, I'm really…" He moved in closer, his hand on the wall beside her head. She swallowed hard, then continued, "sorry that I…slept…with…"

His lips were on hers at the same time her hands cupped his shoulders, squeezing them for dear life. His lips tasted like the ocean, but his warm tongue on hers tasted like him…all man and all need. He pressed his hips into hers for just a moment, and then pulled away. "Sorry, I don't want to get you wet."

His hands slipped up under her shirt and cupped her waist, moving up her torso and to her breasts. Sliding them around to her back, he unhooked her bra and then ran his hands over her bare breasts, her nipples so tight they could poke out an eye.

Lifting her shirt, he reached down and kissed her bare belly, his tongue flickering onto her skin and then moving onto the next spot. She rested against the wall, knowing there should be a protest in her somewhere, but damned if she could find it.

He stood up straight, kissing her again. She realized they may be the exact same height. He was barefooted and she was wearing flat sandals, and they stood exactly evenly matched. He pulled away, his mouth open as he panted. "Can I take you to my bed?"

"Ye—" She stopped herself. "No," she said, her disappointment at her own words consuming her. She ran her hand through her hair as he backed away. "I just came to…I came to…" She glanced around, not a clue why she was there.

"Make the cookie delivery," he supplied.

She snapped. "Yes. That's it. The cookie delivery.

I need to get back to the shop now, and get on with my life, and let you get on with yours." She motioned toward the bar awkwardly.

He stepped back again, and she moved away from the wall, gathering her bearings.

He pointed at her breasts. "Um, may I?"

She stared at him, wide-eyed. "Oh, God, yes. Please." She started to turn around so he could hook her bra back up, but he slid his hands under her shirt from the front and gathered her bra straps, hooking them together around her back. When he finished, he smoothed her shirt down around her waist, and then stepped back, opening the door.

"Thank you," she said, and then walked through.

Kelly the server sped by with two drinks in her hands and a smile on her face. "See you later!"

Cassidy grinned like a maniac and headed to the front door.

Chapter Seven

When Cassidy got to the shop and came through the double swinging doors from the back, Sebastian was at the counter with Marigold. "There's the lovely Cassidy Anderson of Seaside, Florida," he said. "We were just talking about you."

Cassidy slid Marigold a death glare, and she just shrugged back all innocently.

"Okay," Sebastian said, "I was asking her if you'd seen *Till Life Do Us Part* yet, but apparently there's something else I should know. What's going on with the two of you?"

"Nothing," Cassidy said.

Marigold picked up the cleaner and a roll of paper towels. "I'm just going to do the tables."

Sebastian stared at Cassidy like he was trying to see through to her brain. "My goodness, I go out of town for one measly weekend and I miss something epic. What's going on with you?"

She gathered her hair to put back in a ponytail. "Oh, nothing. I'm just losing my mind."

"Yeah, well, I'm sane for the moment, so let me help you. What is all this?" Sebastian had been one of Cassidy's closest friends for about five years now. She hosted him for Thanksgiving at her home every year and had even been known to take him back to Nashville with her for Christmas when he'd agree to go. He had no family that he wanted to speak of. They were more brother and sister than store owner and customer, which was how they'd met. He'd not missed a day stopping by her bakery, assuming he was in town, in five years. He was her perpetual single ally. They'd nursed one another through countless bad dates and crises. So why was she trying so hard to shut him out now?

Marigold cut her glance at them, hovering close. Cassidy rolled her eyes. "Just get over here." Marigold grinned and scooted over to plant herself next to Sebastian.

Cassidy covered her eyes and mouth with her hands. "So I did something a little out of character."

"What was that, hon?" Sebastian asked. "I can't understand you. You sound like Charlie Brown's teacher."

Cassidy removed her hands from her face and repeated, "I did something out of character," the words booming through the store. She couldn't even look at Marigold. Before Dane came along, Cassidy hadn't known Marigold to have sex with anyone in the years she'd known her, much less a one-night-stand.

Marigold rested her elbow on the counter, leaning

in. "With Jesse?" she asked, delicately.

Sebastian gripped the countertop. "Hang on. Do you mean Dane's friend Jesse, the tattooed hunk of divinity who's got that hippy bar in Grayton?"

They both looked at Cassidy for clarification, and she nodded shamefully.

Sebastian closed his eyes and held up a hand like he was in a praise and worship service. "I need a minute."

"It all happened really fast." Cassidy looked around, even though there wasn't a soul in there other than them. "I just got carried away."

They both leaned in on the countertop. "How carried away?" they asked in unison.

Cassidy rubbed her temple. "We were on the beach, and there was wine and—"

"Hang on," Sebastian said. "You had sex on the beach?"

Cassidy gave him a guilty look. "I'm not proud."

"You should be," Marigold said.

"That's not even the worse part. I was so freaked out after it was over that I practically bolted back to the house and kicked him to the curb."

"Aww," Sebastian said, making a frowny face.

"So I go over there today to do the cookie delivery and give some sort of loose apology, and we get started up again."

"You just had sex with him again?" Marigold shouted.

Cassidy cringed. "No, but we were in the stairwell, and he was coming in from the beach and he had these literary tattoos on his torso."

Sebastian bit his fist. "Brains, too. I can't take it."

"So what's the problem?" Marigold asked.

"The problem is I can't get mixed up with this young guy."

"Why the hell not?" Sebastian asked.

Cassidy thought about Todd and their group in Jamaica. Those people were so enlightened, so dedicated to making the world a better place. As much as she hated to admit it, she'd be ashamed if they saw her back here in privileged Seaside, luxuriating in an affair with a twenty-something kid while they were off sleeping on cots and helping improve the lives of those less fortunate. The guilt was starting to strangle her.

"It's just embarrassing. I'm forty-four. What's the point?"

"The point is to have your mind blown," Marigold said.

"There's just other things I could be doing."

"Like going to the movies with me?" Sebastian asked.

Cassidy pointed at him. "Yes. Exactly."

"I was kidding," Sebastian said. "If I ever find out that you are sitting in a theater with me when you could be in bed with that man, I'll murder you."

"Me, too," Marigold said.

Cassidy caught sight of one of the Harrison Pool Supply trucks pulling up out front. "Oh, crap. That's one of the Harrisons. She pointed at the two of them. "Not a word about this to anyone. Do the two of you hear me?"

Sebastian zipped his lip and then handed Marigold an imaginary key that she pretended to swallow. Cassidy shook her head at these two chickens who she loved more than life.

Shayla opened the door to the shop, rocking a Harrison Pool Supply polo and shorts. She could try all she wanted not to impress, but she would always be one of the most stunning people on earth. She smiled at the three of them. "I guess I picked the right time to come by," she said, wrapping her arms around each of them. "What are you three up to?"

Sebastian pulled out his wallet. "Just headed to the nursing home. Since it's almost lunchtime, let's do brownies and cookies today instead of cinnamon rolls."

Marigold scooted around the counter. "I've got this."

They were trying a little too hard to act natural, but Cassidy had to love them for it.

Shayla looked a little confused but seemed to blow it off. She met Cassidy's gaze. "I actually came here to talk to you if you have a minute."

"I do. You want to step into my office?" Cassidy asked, indicating the double swinging doors.

Shayla followed her in there, and they each took a stool by the countertop. "So, I didn't want to make a big deal out of it the other night, but..." Shayla flashed her left hand and then covered it with her right. Shayla was one of the most practical and down-to-earth people on the planet, and she'd had the misfortune of being paired with a man who had money coming out his ears and loved to spend it, poor girl.

Cassidy grinned at her. "Can I see it?"

Shayla reluctantly showed Cassidy her left hand. To Chase's credit, the diamond was simple but stunning. "It's beautiful, Shayla."

She looked at it and then covered it again. "I know it could be worse. I think it killed him to hold back even this much."

"I'm sure he'll live through it."

"I'll get used to it. It's just gonna take some time. I may be one of these women who just wears a band and then pulls out the ring on special occasions."

"Nothing wrong with that."

"Anyway, the wedding's going to be really small. Just family at my parents' house."

"That sounds lovely."

"Thanks. I hope no one is offended by that. It's just…you know me. Can you imagine me in front of a big group of people with a wedding dress on reciting vows?"

Cassidy just smiled her response.

"Anyway, we both want our friends to be some part of all this. Honest to God, you all are as much our family as our actual families are."

Cassidy nodded. "I feel the same."

Shayla gave her a look. "So, while my idea was to have a cookout and a toast and be done with it, Chase has more grandiose plans."

"Okay," Cassidy said.

"He wants to take everyone away for a weekend trip on us. Of course, if it was up to him, we'd all be going to Hawaii or Fiji or Turks and Caicos. But I talked him down to this resort in South Florida that I think will work for all of us. It's not very far away. I know everyone can't be gone from work too long." She offered a hand toward Cassidy. "We're even doing a Saturday to a Monday instead of a Friday, so

I'm hoping that could make this doable for you? The shop's closed on Sundays and Mondays, right?"

"Oh, gosh, you all didn't plan that around me, did you?"

"No, not at all. Fridays are Bo's and my busiest days."

"You're not taking a honeymoon?"

"Not right now. There's just too much going on. But we will. Anyway, please think about whether or not you could close the shop for a Saturday. We'd love to have both you and Marigold there. Of course, Mr. Moneypants offered to pay you for lost profits for the day." Even though she rolled her eyes, Cassidy could tell Shayla was gauging her to see if she might consider taking the money.

Cassidy chuckled. "Only Chase O'Neil would offer to take someone away for the weekend and pay them for it."

"Right?" Shayla asked, shaking her head. "Anyway, just think about it. We'd love to have you there, but we understand life goes on whether or not the two of us get married."

Cassidy smiled. "I don't have to think about it. It's a done deal. When will it be?"

She winced. "We're looking at next weekend. I know that's super short notice, but it's the only weekend that's working with our schedules. Bo and Maya and Seanna and Blake are already confirmed. I'm going to hit up Sebastian if he's still out there when we're through. I think Chase is checking with Dane and Ashe and Ethan today. I'm stopping by Desiree's office right after this."

"Is that everyone?" Cassidy asked.

"For now, but you know Chase. Before this is over, he's liable to have invited every stray dog and cat east of Pensacola."

"Understood."

Shayla touched Cassidy's knee. "And you are more than welcome to bring a date."

"Oh, God no. Put me and Sebastian in a room. We've bunked together several times on trips. We're great roommates."

"Thanks for the offer, but Chase would be mortified to ask people to bunk up. I'm warning you, he's gonna go all out on this trip." She scratched her forehead. "It makes me a little uncomfortable."

"Sweetheart, all of these people know Chase. Nobody thinks he's showing off, I promise you that. He's purely generous. We all know that, and we appreciate him."

Shayla smiled. "Thanks for saying that."

"How are we getting there, by the way?"

Shayla winced. "Private plane. Chase swears he's getting a great deal and that it's gonna be cheaper than flying everyone commercial."

"Do you believe him?"

"Hell, no."

Cassidy laughed, and Shayla checked the time on her phone. "I better go. My mean-ass brother will get antsy if I'm gone too long from the shop."

Cassidy loved the relationship between Shayla and Bo. They had each other's back like no siblings Cassidy had ever known. Cassidy and her sister weren't nearly as tight as that. As much as she wished things could be different, she knew that was just the way it went for her and her family.

They both stood, and Cassidy and Shayla wrapped their arms around one another. "Love you, girl," Cassidy said. She pulled away, holding Shayla's shoulders. "Congratulations are for the groom, so I'll just say best wishes."

Shayla smiled. "Thanks. Honestly, I can't wait for it all to be over. I hate being the center of attention."

"Well, I'm afraid once Marigold gets wind of this she's gonna have some plans for this weekend that may require a tiara and a white sash with the word bride in all caps."

Shayla waved Cassidy off. "I've already thought of that. She can have at it. Dress me in a tutu if she wants." They both looked out to the front where Marigold was chatting up a customer. "I'm just so thankful to have friends who love me like you all do." She turned to Cassidy, her eyes a little glassy. "You know, that's a rare thing."

Cassidy felt the pressure building up behind her own eyes. "I know it is." They took one another's hands and squeezed them hard.

Shayla swiped at her eyes. "Oh crap. It's already starting."

Cassidy chuckled. "Get ready. As soon as you tell Marigold about this weekend, you'll be unleashing a beast."

Shayla shook her head and then stood tall, ready for battle. "Bring on the penis-shaped piñata."

Chapter Eight

Jesse set glasses of draft beer down in front of Dane, Chase, Bo, and Blake. "Have you guys decided what you want to eat?"

"It's your bar, man," Chase said. "You know better than us."

Jesse was proud of his place, but this guy was rolling in it, apparently. He was probably used to eating a lot better than this.

Dane picked up the cards he'd just been dealt. "Everything here's good. I'm a big fan of the oysters though."

"Then bring us four plates of those," Chase said, "and anything else you've got too much of back there."

"Are you gonna play with us?" Blake asked.

Dane shrugged at Jesse. When Dane had asked him if they could do this poker night in his private room, he'd told Jesse it was the first time he'd been asked. He wasn't sure how strict these guys were with their rules. Dane was only in because their regular fourth had bailed.

"Can you get away?" Chase asked.

Jesse glanced out at the main floor. They were busy but not slammed. "Maybe for a round or two."

"We're damn sure not gonna turn down your money," Bo said. "Join us."

Jesse wouldn't mind getting an in with these guys who were Cassidy's friends. It'd been a week since she'd run a finger over his tattoo, drawing him to her like a siren. He'd not had the balls to text her, especially after her comment about getting on with her life. He could keep coming on strong, and might be able to get her to sleep with him again, but that wasn't what he wanted. He wanted her to want to get to know him for more than whatever fascination she had with his looks or his youth. He hoped hearing that he liked to read might pique her interest, but he'd not heard another word from her. He knew he should give up, but he wasn't ready to. And he hadn't figured out a way forward yet.

"Let me put in an order for the food," he said and headed to the kitchen. When he returned, a pile of cards sat in front of an empty chair one of them had pulled over. How could these guys make him feel so welcome in his own bar?

Jesse listened and observed for a few rounds, letting them engage in their easy conversation and banter with one another. They liked to give each other shit. The harder core, the better.

Bo eyed Jesse, and he felt it coming. He was a little surprised it had taken Bo this long. "So, have you taken Cassidy out yet?"

Dane met Jesse's gaze with a knowing look. What had he and Marigold been talking about? Did Dane know something he wasn't sharing with him? He'd have to beat it out of him in a bit. Jesse looked at Blake to see if he was going to play good cop again tonight, but he just stared at his cards. Maybe his curiosity was getting the best of him, too.

Jesse moved some cards around in his hand. "This seems to be a subject you can't drop."

Bo shrugged. "Just making conversation."

Chase smiled. "It's killing him because he could never land her."

"I'm sorry," Bo said, putting his cards on the table face down. "I'm a very happily married man, in case you haven't noticed."

Blake snickered. "Doesn't mean you're not competitive."

Bo sat back, glaring at Chase and Blake. "I'm ashamed of the two of you, indicating that I would actually care who Cassidy dated, other than making sure she wasn't being mistreated, of course." With that, Bo gave a pointed glance to Jesse.

Jesse slid his gaze to Dane, who just smiled while staring at his cards.

Chase motioned at Bo. "Please, will you just admit you're dying to know what he's got that you don't?"

Bo slid his chair back. "I will take your ass out right here if you don't shut the hell up."

Chase, who was at least half a foot taller than Bo, looked completely unfazed at this threat.

"I think there's a story we're missing out on, Jesse," Dane said.

"Definitely," Jesse said.

Blake grinned. "She kicked his ass once."

Bo gave Blake an exhausted look. "Now why would you say that when you know it's not true?"

"It's not?" Blake asked, eyebrows raised.

Bo pouted a little as he picked up his cards. "She punched me. She did not kick my ass."

Dane and Jesse met each other's gazes and cracked up along with the rest of the table except for Bo. Damn, she hit Bo? At least she hadn't punched Jesse. #winning

Finally, Bo dropped his cards again, a smile making its way across his face. "Fuck it. I'm impressed, okay? How'd you get her interested?"

Jesse didn't know how to handle this. He now had four sets of eyes on him, waiting for a response to how he landed Cassidy when he wasn't even near the landing strip. He shrugged. "I'm not sure what you mean."

"Oh, please," Bo said. "I saw you two coming in from my backyard the other night. You looked like two kids who got caught with their hands in the cookie jar."

Jesse shrugged. "She's cool. I like her."

"Well, duh, you like her," Bo said. "Every man who meets her likes her. You think you're special?"

Jesse glanced around the table, all of them seeming in agreement. He met Blake's gaze. "Did you have a thing for her?"

"For about a week. But then she was the first friend I made here and I didn't want to fuck that up. Not that she'd have been interested."

"You?" Jesse asked Chase.

"I thought she was hot, for sure, but I knew Bo had a thing for her, so I didn't even consider it."

Bo gave him a look that might have constituted a thank you.

Jesse turned to Dane. "You?"

"I met her at the same time I met Marigold, so I had my sights set elsewhere. But yeah, I was definitely intrigued."

Damn. Jesse had no idea he was such a cliché. He considered Bo from across the table. Bo was a good-looking guy, buff, masculine...the kind of guy women typically went for. What had been her holdup with him? "So why didn't it work out between the two of you?"

"She doesn't date younger guys," Blake said. "Well, not typically."

Jesse wasn't sure if he should be surprised by that statement or not.

"But apparently she's making an exception for Jesse," Chase said, and Bo just pursed his lips.

"I wasn't aware the two of you were dating," Dane said, giving Jesse a look.

Jesse gleaned that Dane knew more than he'd communicated to him yet, and that he needed to wrap this shit up. Bo and Blake may have their brotherly telepathic connection, but Dane and Jesse had their own version of that, too.

Jesse picked his cards up. "We're not dating."

"Really?" Chase asked.

"Really."

"But you're interested," Bo stated.

Jesse met Dane's gaze, who gave him the slightest shake of his head. Jesse sat back, "Well, like you all said, she's hot, but she's not interested in younger guys. And I'm definitely a younger guy. Younger than the three of you for sure." He indicated all but Dane.

"Are you calling me an old man?" Bo asked.

"What are you? Fifty-three, fifty-four?"

Bo's glare morphed into a smile. "Go get some more money out of your register. You're getting ready to need it."

Jesse smiled along with the rest of the guys. He wasn't sure, but he might have just passed some sort of initiation into this group of friends.

Jesse saw the guys out, Dane hanging back, saying he needed to hit the head. When he came out, Jesse met him at the bar.

Dane hiked his leg over a barstool. "Well, what did you think?"

"I think they're fucking nuts."

Dane smiled. "Yeah, I like them, too."

"You want a Coke or another beer?"

"Coke. Thanks."

Jesse poured him one into a plastic cup and handed it to him. "So what do you know that you're not telling me?"

"It's not that I'm not telling you. It's just…when have we talked last?"

That was Jesse's fault. Their relationship was lopsided. They remained friends through the years because Dane put forth all the effort. He made it a habit to eat lunch there at least a couple of days a week or stop by after work for a beer. If Dane quit coming, Jesse wondered if he'd make the effort to keep in touch. Jesse's whole world was the bar. His friends were his patrons. He'd lost touch with everyone he'd ever known. Social media wasn't his thing. He'd never been one to want to display his life, but more than that, he didn't want to see other people's lives playing out when he had specifically distanced himself from them.

Jesse leaned onto the bar. "What has she told Marigold about me?"

Dane lifted an eyebrow. "I'm not supposed to say."

Jesse pulled away, gripping the bar. "What the fuck, man? Are you gonna be one of those guys who's more loyal to your woman than you are to your best friend?"

"Hell yeah," Dane said.

"Fuck you."

Dane held up his drink in a cheers motion and took a sip.

"Come on, man. I'm dying here."

"Dying? Really?"

"Theoretically speaking."

Dane narrowed his gaze. "So, you're really into her, huh?"

If Jesse wanted information, he was going to have to give some. He understood this. He didn't like it, but he got it. He leaned back in. "I'm going ballistic over here. I can't quit thinking about her. I've slept with more women these past few years than I should admit to, but I can't get this one off my brain. I think about her all the time, and I don't even know her, but I'm dying to."

Dane nodded as if this all made perfect sense, but

kept tight-lipped.

"What has she said about me, man? Give me a hint."

"I don't necessarily know what she's said. I just know what Marigold has observed."

Jesse lifted an eyebrow. "And?"

Dane pursed his lips, looking down at his drink.

"Just answer this," Jesse said. "Should I keep trying, or do I need to back off?"

Dane glanced around the room like they were exchanging top secret information. He met Jesse's intent gaze. "Keep trying."

Jesse's chest lit up, and a smile crept across his lips that he couldn't contain. The door opened, and Chase walked in. "Hey, man," Jesse said, waving him over to the bar. "Did you forget something?"

He headed that way. "Nah, I've just been outside bullshitting with them. Bo wouldn't shut the hell up."

Jesse nodded with a smile.

Chase backhanded Dane on the shoulder. "Have you told him about this weekend?"

"No, I haven't," Dane said.

"Shayla and I are taking a bunch of our friends to this swanky resort in South Florida. It's to celebrate us getting married. We'd love you to come. Dane's coming, aren't you?"

"Yep," Dane said, holding back a smile.

"It's this coming weekend. I know that's short notice, but if you can get away…" His eyebrows went up in a question.

Jesse looked around his bar that ran like a well-oiled machine thanks to his currently reliable staff. He looked at Dane whose eyes went wide, encouragingly.

"Are you sure?" Jesse asked.

Chase smiled. "Cassidy's gonna be there."

A weekend away with Cassidy—what had he done to deserve this? "You don't think Bo would mind me being there?" Jesse asked.

"The thing to know about Bo is the more shit he gives you, the more he likes you."

Dane cut his eyes at Jesse. "He must be in love with you then."

Chase nodded confirmation. "He's fine with it. It was his idea, actually."

"Really?" Jesse asked.

"Swear to God. Just now out on the sidewalk." Chase reached across the bar and backhanded him on the shoulder. "Come. We'd love to have you."

Jesse couldn't believe his fortune. "Thanks. I think I will."

"Great." Chase got out his phone. "What's your number? I'm gonna text you my assistant's number. Text her your address and she'll arrange to have you picked up on Saturday morning. It's from Saturday to Monday. Does that work for you?"

"I think it will." Jesse rattled off his number.

"Cool." Chase pocketed his phone. "I'll see you both on Saturday," he said with a wink and headed out.

Jesse turned back to Dane who said, "I guess we're both in."

"I guess so. Is that a good thing or bad?"

Dane stood up off the stool. "We'll know after this weekend."

Chapter Nine

Cassidy felt like royalty as she shook hands with the pilot and flight attendant who stood at the bottom of the staircase that led up to the private plane. Due to some mix-up with the limos, Cassidy had ridden in one all by herself. She knew they were going *wheels up* at nine-thirty, and it was just about that time, but she'd been at the mercy of a slow as molasses limo driver.

"Welcome aboard," the very handsome pilot said to her.

"Am I the last to arrive?" she asked.

"Yes, ma'am, but there's an empty seat waiting for you. Last one."

"I hope I didn't hold you all up."

"Not at all," the flight attendant said with a smile. He was good-looking as well. Was that a requirement on this particular charter service?

She shouldered her purse as she ascended the

stairs, telling herself to remember this weekend because she'd never have another one like it. That was for sure. As she rounded the corner, Chase and Shayla greeted her from the two front seats.

"Hey, girl," Shayla said with a smile about as wide as Cassidy had ever seen from her. Shayla was chill pretty much all the time, but a weekend as grandiose as this one called for a smile as big as that one.

Cassidy hugged both Shayla and Chase. "My own private limo?" she said to Chase. "You're gonna have me so spoiled before this weekend's over I'm not gonna know what to do with myself."

"It's more fun for me than for you all, trust me. I love it," Chase said, and she believed him.

Cassidy glanced around the plane, which had a single row of seats on one side and a row of double seats on the other.

"Just head on down the aisle. There's an empty seat for you down the way." He pointed at the one next to them. "I think the flight attendant uses that one."

"All right," Cassidy said, glancing down the single row which looked fairly full at a glance.

Row two housed Desiree and her on-and-off-again boyfriend Tobias, with Ashe in the single seat. The next row had Marigold and Dane on one side with Ethan, Dane's twin brother, in the single. The next row had Bo and Maya on one side with Sebastian on his own, and the next row had...

Cassidy stopped in her tracks as she caught sight of Jesse sitting against the window with a stunning young woman sitting next to him, hanging on his every word.

This was it. Her own personal hell. Jesse, who she'd slept with on the beach two weeks ago, and who had not begun to leave her brain and her nonstop fantasies, had been dating a beautiful young girl his own age, and had brought her on this trip. This is what she got for acting like a fool. Stupid was as stupid did, as her mom so often repeated to her and her sister.

"Cassidy!" came Seanna's voice. She stood from the seats behind Jesse and his lovely date, and rounded the seat, wrapping her arms around Cassidy in a hug. She pulled away. "I'm so excited that you're here. I was afraid you wouldn't want to close the shop."

And to think, she'd have had the perfect excuse to get out of this nightmare. "It was just for the day," Cassidy said, making eye contact with Jesse's date, who was suddenly very interested in her and smiling from ear to ear. Oh God. Did she have to be kind and cordial, too?

Seanna looked down at her. "Cassidy, I want you to meet someone. This is my assistant, Hannah."

The girl stood, taking Cassidy's hand and covering it with her other one. "I am so excited to finally meet you. Seanna talks about you all the time. She absolutely adores you."

Cassidy glanced at Jesse, whose attention was on his phone. She met Hannah's kind gaze. "Yes, Hannah. Seanna has mentioned you as well," Cassidy lied. She wasn't even sure she knew Seanna had hired an assistant.

"I'm very much looking forward to getting to

know you this weekend," Hannah said.

"If everyone could please get seated, we're going to take off in just a bit," said an authoritative but friendly voice over an intercom system.

Hannah shook Jesse's hand. "So nice to meet you, Jesse." She turned to Cassidy with her winning smile and grinned with a little wave as she scooted to the single seat in the row with Seanna and Blake. Cassidy glanced at the single seat in Jesse's row, which held a young woman with earbuds whom she didn't recognize.

The woman met her gaze with a kind but business-like smile, taking one earbud out. "I'm Chase's assistant Megan. Working trip."

"Cassidy," she replied, and the girl gave her a firm handshake, then put her earbud back in.

Jesse met Cassidy's gaze and then looked down at the seat. "I think I'm your only choice."

A glance at the back of the plane confirmed that he was correct. There were a few more seats, but they were all occupied by people Cassidy didn't know.

"That's another group who Chase split the charter with. I think they're headed to Key West after they drop us off."

"Ah," Cassidy said, plopping down next to him, wondering how many emotions she could experience in one brief stint of time.

Cassidy felt a hand on her shoulder and turned to find Hannah leaned toward her. "I adore your top by the way. Free People?" she asked.

Cassidy glanced down at it. "Oh, um, I doubt it. I think it came from a sale rack somewhere."

The girl smiled. "Even better." She sat back and

started going through her purse.

Cassidy turned to Jesse, who was looking at the girl and then met Cassidy's gaze. "Oh, wait," Jesse said. "Did you think she was my date?"

Cassidy just dropped her head to the side.

"I can see why you thought that with her sitting here with me. But no. I just met her." He grinned, an over-the-top gesture to drive home his humiliating point.

"I wasn't thinking anything about it at all, actually," she said, pulling her magazine out of her purse and then shoving her purse under the seat in front of them.

"No, of course you weren't. You're getting on with your life."

She winced, remembering her words from a week and a half ago.

"You didn't want to bring a date?" he asked her.

"I'm not dating anyone," she said, flipping a page on her magazine.

"Yeah, I'm not either. Well, there is this one girl I keep bumping into, but she's not really interested. I mean," he leaned in close, "we had this one incredible night together, but she's made it clear since then that she has no interest in moving things forward, which is really a shame, because there's so much I still want to know about her."

Heat filled Cassidy's chest and ran up through her neck, her stomach buzzing.

The flight attendant interrupted with his preflight spiel, and Jesse opened the book he'd been holding in his lap. Cassidy glanced around the plane with an unreasonable fear that all these people knew or suspected her business. But Megan sat across the aisle from her intently listening to whatever was coming through her earbuds as she stared out the window. Sebastian in the seat in front of her knew all about it but loved Cassidy anyway. She glanced over the seat back to find Blake and Seanna disgustingly nuzzling into one another with grins. Clearly they couldn't care less what Cassidy was doing. Maybe she just needed to get over herself and realize that she wasn't all that interesting to these people after all.

Jesse flipped a page in his book. Was he really reading? How could he lay something like that on her, and then happily start reading his book, focused and comprehending? She damn sure couldn't.

The plane made its ascension into the air, and Jesse stared out the window. "That never gets old to me. The amazement that this machine can lift up into the air, defying gravity. I mean, I know it's plain and simple aerodynamics, but it's still amazing to me. I don't care how naïve that makes me sound."

Cassidy smiled, because she'd always thought the same thing. "It's a shame to me when I'm on a flight and I see all these people staring into their phones or with their eyes closed, seeming completely disinterested when we're literally passing through clouds. It seems unreal."

He nodded, still looking out the window. She found herself pulled toward the window, and him. When the plane leveled out, he turned toward her, and they were so close they almost kissed by accident.

She fell back into her seat. "Sorry."

"For what?"

"Invading your space."

"I think we're past that, don't you?"

She leaned toward the aisle, scratching her forehead, heat rising up to her ears. She could feel his eyes on her, studying her.

"Do I embarrass you?" he asked.

"What?" she said, meeting his gaze.

"You turn red a lot. You didn't do that the first couple of times I met you, but ever since—"

She held a finger to her lips, sinking down in her seat a little. Megan, in the seat next to them, remained uninterested, thankfully.

"Hang on," he said, sitting back away from her. "I don't embarrass you. You're embarrassed *of* me."

She let her head fall to the side. "Don't be ridiculous." Was he being ridiculous?

He nodded, a sardonic smile on his face. "Okay, I see how it is."

She touched his arm. "I'm not embarrassed of you," she said, keeping her voice way down.

He put his hand to his ear. "Hmm? What's that? I can't hear you."

She gave him a look. "I'm not embarrassed of you," she said, louder, but still where nobody else around them could hear, hopefully.

He narrowed his gaze at her. "So I hear you don't date younger guys."

She blinked. "Where would you have heard that from?"

"Chase. Or was it Blake? One of them. They were at the bar the other night for their card game."

A small panic rose in her chest. "And you all were talking about me?"

"You seem to come up frequently with Bo. He's very concerned about what's going on with you and me."

"What did you tell him?"

It was his turn to drop his head to the side. "Will you give me some credit?"

Her panic subsided a little. She still didn't know Jesse well enough to gauge whether or not he was lying. But he seemed sincere.

"Would that be the worst thing in the world if these people found out we slept together?"

She rested her elbow on the armrest beside her, pinching the bridge of her nose. "Can we just table this discussion, please?"

He put his attention back on his book. "No problem."

God she was messing this up, so epically. She put her hand on his arm. "I'm not embarrassed of you. I'm embarrassed of myself and my actions, okay?"

He squinted at her. "Because you slept with me?"

She closed her eyes, trying to think of a way to explain this to him. "Because I'm not myself when I'm around you. I become someone I don't recognize. I'm typically very in control with the men I date…not that you could call what's been happening between us dating, but regardless, I'm not in control around you. I become this other version of myself that quite frankly scares me."

"You don't seem very scary to me."

She smiled, looking down at her lap. "No, I imagine I do not."

"You seem intimidating, but not scary."

She jerked her head up. "Intimidating? You can't

be serious."

He shifted his body to face her. "Are you fucking kidding me?" he said, keeping his volume in check. "You're this sophisticated, mature, beautiful woman who runs her own business and does long-term volunteer work and feels guilty because you don't do more. Everyone in your orbit worships you. You should have heard those guys talking about you the other night. Do you have a clue what people think about you? They look up to you. They want to be you and they want to be with you. I'm just trying to figure out how the hell I broke down your wall, even if it was just for one night."

A monsoon of emotions swirled inside her mind, unworthiness and humility rising to the top. She looked away from him, putting her attention onto the magazine in her lap that she couldn't read if she tried. She rested her cheek in her hand and let her mass of hair fall down the right side of her face so she couldn't see him next to her. But she could feel him there. Jesus, how she could feel his presence.

Chapter Ten

Jesse and Cassidy stood in separate lines for check in, both flipping through their phones, but Jesse couldn't help glances in her direction. He'd fucked up again, saying way too much. He couldn't help it. He had no idea how to behave around this woman. She didn't operate like any other girl he'd been with before. Whatever game plan he thought he'd brought this weekend needed to be reconfigured, because at this rate, he'd be leaving there not having gotten to know her any better than he did before he'd arrived.

They both moved up to the counter at roughly the same time, giving their information.

"O'Neil party?" the girl behind the counter said to Jesse with a lift of her eyebrow and a grin.

"Yep," he said, glancing at Cassidy.

"Just you in the room?" the girl asked.

"Uh, yeah. Just me."

She smiled with a nod, brushing a lock of hair

behind her ear. Jesse knew this to be the international mating sign for women. Everything about this girl shouted that she was interested. This is where he'd make a suggestive joke and then gauge her reaction. If that went well, he'd ask her what there was to do around there. Depending on that reaction, he'd ask if she wanted to do it with him. Then they'd be off. But the problem was, he couldn't quit glancing over at Cassidy.

She slid a key card to him. "Here's your key. I'm right here till three if you have any questions."

He took the card from her. "I'll keep that in mind."

She smiled again, and he stepped away and headed toward the elevator, shouldering his bag. Cassidy came his way, dragging a small suitcase on rollers. The two of them stood by the elevators in silence, Jesse's heartbeat pounding harder than normal. Just having her in his vicinity did that to him.

The elevator doors opened and the two of them got on. Part of him hoped someone else would join them, and the other part wished he could be alone with her from now until the end of the weekend. She hit the button for floor four, and he smiled. She met his gaze. "What floor do you need?"

He nodded at the button. "Same as you."

She glanced down at her phone, resting against the elevator wall. He wished he could see her face, but her hair was always covering it.

Both of their phones dinged at the same time, and she read the text aloud. "We're meeting down in the lobby in a half hour for lunch by the pool."

"Sounds like a plan," he said.

The elevator stopped and he motioned for her to get off first, and then he followed her out. He stopped at his room. "See you in a bit."

She checked something in her hand and closed her eyes, but stayed right beside him. She cut her gaze at him and pointed at the door next to his. "This is me."

He had done something right after all. "Hope you don't snore too loud." He pushed open his door and grinned as he spotted a connecting door that led to her room.

When Jesse got down to the pool, Cassidy was sitting at a table with a handful of people he hadn't met yet—a black couple and a guy he'd seen Cassidy sitting with the night of her welcome back party at his bar a few weeks ago. But it was pretty clear she wasn't romantically interested in him. He seemed like he was probably gay. Jesse couldn't be sure, because straight men his age could be ambiguous. But either way, Cassidy didn't seem interested in more than friendship.

Dane waved him over to his table with Marigold, Ashe, and Ethan. A fifth chair was positioned awkwardly between Dane and Ethan. They'd likely pulled it over for him. Jesse hated that Dane felt like he needed to babysit him this weekend, but he was glad to be included, especially since he didn't really know any of these people.

"We got a few apps for the table," Dane said. "You know Ashe, right?"

Jesse shook the guy's hand. He had a subtle glam rock vibe to him. Jesse had never gone the guy route, but he could see why Ethan was into him. "We may have met a few weeks ago when you all were at the bar for Cassidy's welcome home party."

"Yes, we definitely met then," Ashe said, squeezing Jesse's hand with a lingering gaze.

"Uh, hello. Remember me?" Ethan said, and Ashe gave him a quick kiss on the mouth.

"Speaking of Cassidy," Ashe said, "I saw you two sitting together on the plane. Are you an item?"

Marigold and Dane exchanged a look and then got interested in their drinks.

"No, she just had the misfortune of taking the last open seat next to me."

"I'd have been glad to take it," Ashe said, and then turned to Ethan. "Before you, sweetie. I'm just playing with the straight boy."

Ethan rolled his eyes lovingly as if he dealt with this all the time.

"How do you know I'm straight?" Jesse asked, playing along for fun.

Ashe lifted an eyebrow and the server appeared next to Jesse. "What can I get you to drink?"

Jesse ordered a beer, and another server came up behind them with plates of food. "Looks like I timed my entrance just right," Jesse said.

"Happy we could be of service," Ashe said. Jesse knew he was in for a ride with this guy this weekend. That was okay. He liked to flirt. Besides, the way he and Ethan looked at one another, Jesse knew he wasn't any threat to this couple.

As they were finishing eating, Cassidy and her friends stood. The white guy that had been at their table headed back into the hotel, but the other three went toward the pool, pausing at Jesse's group. The woman he hadn't met yet rubbed Ashe's shoulders. "You all having fun yet?"

"Always," Marigold said. "Have you met Jesse?"

"No, I don't think so." She offered a long, slim hand. "I'm Desiree, and this is Tobias."

Jesse shook hands with both of them. "Nice to meet you."

She pointed to the far side of the pool. "Chase has us in those two cabanas on the end. Y'all come on over when you're done."

"We'll be right there," Ashe said.

Cassidy met Jesse's gaze with a hint of a smile. She wore a one-piece bathing suit with a pair of shorts and a sheer cover-up. She would have to shed some of those clothes eventually, and that was a sight he was looking forward to seeing.

After they finished and tried to pay—Chase, though not in sight anywhere, had already taken care of the bill—they headed over to the cabana. The lounge chairs were stacked in rows paired off in twos. Four under the shade and four out in the sun. Desiree and her man sat under the shade, and Marigold and Dane took the empty seats next to them. Ethan and Ashe set their bags on a pair of seats in the sun. "We're going exploring," Ethan said.

Cassidy sat in the sun in the front row. She'd shed her cover-up and shorts, leaving her long, lean body on beautiful display. Even with the one-piece she looked better than any other girl around. She indicated the only empty chair which was beside her. "Please, sit."

"Where's your other friend?" Jesse asked.

"Sebastian went back to his room. He's in the

middle of a work project. He'll be down later for dinner."

He grabbed a towel from a rack next to the cabana. "You don't mind being seen with me?"

She gave him a look. "I'll take my chances."

He laid the towel out on the chair and then sat next to her. She handed him a bottle of spray sunscreen.

"No thanks. I put mine on upstairs."

"Really? How responsible of you."

He shrugged. "I actually put it on every morning. My grandfather died of skin cancer when I was nine. My sister was hardcore about skin protection."

"Your sister?"

He waved her off. "It's a long story."

"We've got a lot of time."

He considered her and then lay back. "My mom and dad divorced when I was seven. Dad moved to Minnesota for a new job, and Mom went into a depression for a while. My sister sort of raised me, in a sense. My mom was there, but even when she pulled out of the funk, she was more interested in dating and finding another husband than parenting. Rachel had always been bossy, so she loved it." He huffed a laugh, remembering. "It didn't go over well when I said I was moving to Florida."

"Where are you from?"

"Louisville, Kentucky."

"I've got friends in Louisville I always threaten to visit but never do. It's just hard to get away."

"How many people do you have working your bakery?" he asked.

"Well, right now it's just Marigold and me, but I'll need some more help this summer. I'm not sure how long Marigold's gonna stick around."

He considered her. "What made you decide to open a bakery?"

She laughed. "I ask myself that all the time. Honestly, I was living out some sort of dream from my childhood. My sister's twelve years older than me. She used to play bakery with me. I had this toy oven that made actual cakes. They were terrible, of course, but I thought that was the coolest thing on the planet. We'd make real cupcakes and wrap them up and sell them to my stuffed animals for a nickel a piece." She shook her head with a smile, looking like she'd escaped to another life.

"Is it all you dreamed it would be?"

She swatted a bug off her arm. "It's fine. It's a living. I like being my own boss. You understand that, I'm sure."

"Sometimes. It's nice when I want to do my thing, but even when I leave to go running or paddleboarding or whatever when it's slow, I feel guilty for slacking off."

"You've earned that right though." She nudged him in the arm. "It's impressive, you running your own business at such a young age."

He frowned at her. "How old do you think I am?"

She scrunched up her face. "Um, twenty-nine."

"Who told you?"

She smiled. "Marigold."

"Tattletale," he said.

She giggled. Damn that was cute. He lifted his shirt off and tossed it between his legs. She directed her attention to the pool and stretched her arm over her head, gripping the pole at the top of the chaise lounge with a grin.

"What?" he asked.

"Nothing."

"It is a pool. Guys typically go shirtless at pools, if you haven't taken a look around lately."

"I didn't say anything."

"You were damn sure thinking something. You only smile like that when you're thinking something."

"Oh yeah? You think you know my smiles already?"

"Oh, I definitely know your smiles."

She looked over at him in challenge. "What smiles?"

"You've got your polite smile. This is the one you give when you think something's moderately funny. It's accompanied by a little nod of your head as you look down. Then there's your smile when you really think something's funny. It stretches all the way across your face and your nose twitches, which is the cutest damned thing I've ever seen. Then there's your embarrassed smile, the one you couldn't stop if you tried. It happens without your permission, I'm guessing, and sometimes that smile lives only in your eyes 'cause you're trying so hard not to give anything away."

She stared at him like she was trying to make her expression impassive, but she couldn't control it. He pointed at her. "See, you're giving that smile now."

She lifted an eyebrow and then put her attention on her phone in her lap, letting her hair fall around her face again.

"And you can try to hide your expression with

your hair, but I see you." Knowing when to leave well-enough alone, he stood up from his chair and walked to the pool, doing a front flip into the water.

Jesus Christ he was good. With each word out of his mouth Cassidy realized just how much he had her nailed, and he didn't even know her yet. How fast and how furious did women fall for this guy? How many hearts had he filled and then emptied when he moved on to the next? She tried to imagine the women he'd said these things to before, and their naïve expressions as they fell hook, line, and sinker. The only gullible face she could see though was her own.

She couldn't help wondering what his game was. He'd already had her. He'd won. But he was still playing for some reason.

Maybe she was a novelty—something different he'd not had before. A toy that intrigued him. Maybe he'd never been with an older woman. He'd mentioned his mom. Maybe there was some issue there and he was working that out. God, please no. The last thing she wanted to do was be a part of someone working out their Oedipus complex.

Jesse rose up from the water, facing her, and ran his hands over his hair, pulling it back. He was almost too hot to digest, the muscles rippling in his tattooed forearms, his bare, empty canvas of a chest dripping with water and bursting with muscle.

She remembered a time that she could land decent looking young guys. She'd been blessed with her father's thin frame, but with it had come his nose. She'd forgiven him for it though, his lucky genes affording her the luxury of a fast metabolism.

The ironic thing with Jesse, who was now tossing a football with some teenage kid in the pool, was that Cassidy typically relied on her appearance to attract men. And the men she dated appreciated her body. She'd always been proud of it and happy to wear tank tops and shorts that really were too short for her age. Not all the time, but to the beach or somewhere casual. But Jesse was used to girls half Cassidy's age. What did she have to impress him with? She imagined the taut, smooth skin of a twenty-something young woman.

On cue, Hannah, Seanna's lovely assistant, walked toward the pool from the other cabana sporting a bikini that could make a grown man cry. Hopping into the water, she held her hands in front of her face, encouraging Jesse to throw her the football, which he did. The teenage boy was all too happy to let Hannah into the game.

Cassidy shifted in her chair, hating that she was doubting herself. Since when did her confidence in her appearance waver? Since she'd let herself get interested in a man half her age...that was when.

Chapter Eleven

Poor Shayla had endured the full bachelorette treatment at the hands of Marigold with everything from a tiara veil to penis straws. Cassidy had seen way worse, and Marigold was a very tasteful woman which helped, but Marigold had ensured they spent two hours making Shayla the absolute center of attention. Shayla protested a little at first, which was expected, but after she settled in, Cassidy might have suspected a little enjoyment on Shayla's part.

At ten o'clock sharp, Shayla shed the veil as she said she would. "Time's up, Cinderella," she said, putting the veil on Marigold's head.

Marigold vogued with it for a moment, and then took it off. "Lord, don't let Dane see me like this. I'm still trying to nab him. The last thing I need is for him to see me playing bride."

Sebastian took the veil from her and put it on his own head. "I'm fairly sure he's nabbed."

"Are we going to where the guys are, or are they coming to us?" Desiree asked. She'd been anxious about leaving Tobias. He'd been around their group a handful of times, but with their on-again-off-again status, the guys of the group were a little suspicious of him. Tobias seemed like he could handle himself though.

Cassidy checked her text. "They're at the dance club at the hotel."

"Perfect," Sebastian said, shedding the veil. "I've had all the fun I can stand for a night."

Marigold grabbed his shoulders. "You're such an old man sometimes, Sebastian."

"I know, princess. But this old man needs his beauty sleep if I'm going to be fit for consumption tomorrow. Besides, we're steering into couple-mode now and…" He held up both hands, glancing around for a nonexistent partner.

Cassidy could not for the life of her understand how some incredibly lucky man had not found his way to Sebastian by now. He was one of the most amazing creatures on earth—the whole perfect package from his appearance to his kind and generous heart. Her own heart pained her when she thought about it.

"I'll poop out with you, Bastian," she said, wrapping her arm around him as they walked toward the limo waiting for them outside.

"Oh, don't you dare." He waggled his eyebrows at her.

She rolled her eyes as they pushed through the double doors. "I can't keep going there."

"Why not, hon? He's so incredibly yummy. Do

you not deserve a little candy once in a while?"

They stopped in front of the limo where their friends were piling in. She glanced around to make sure nobody was listening in, and then leaned in. "I just feel like an idiot. A cougar cliché."

"Oh yes, because all our friends are so judgmental." He gave her a sarcastic lift of the eyebrows.

"Okay then, to myself. What's the goal here? Spend a few nights going nuts and then settle back into my old, tired life?"

"Why does it have to just be a few nights?"

"Oh, come on now, friend. I'm not that naïve. I'm a novelty to that man, a gimmick. When he's done, he'll move on. And I'll be honest, I'm starting to realize he's more than a good-looking face. I don't want to get sucked into whatever it is he puts out there that makes women nuts. I've got to keep my wits."

"Come on, slow pokes," yelled Marigold from inside the limo.

Sebastian held up a finger. "Hold your penis balloons. We'll be right there." He turned back to Cassidy. "I hear you on this. I promise I do. But people like you and I aren't single at our ages because we let people in easily. When's the last time you let yourself fall into a relationship that made absolutely no sense?"

Cassidy huffed a laugh. "I've never done that."

"Just try it out. Give in to whatever will of yours that's holding you back from enjoying some time with this man. You may find this thing taking you somewhere unexpected."

She took his hand and squeezed it. "Have I told you lately how much you mean to me?"

He waved her off. "Get a tattoo so you can quit saying it. Get in, Gisele."

When they arrived at the hotel, they all headed straight for the nightclub, but Cassidy held back with Sebastian. "You're headed upstairs?"

He eyed the nightclub, booming with music. "I'll walk you down there, make sure everyone's behaving. But don't tattle on me if I slip out unnoticed."

"Never," Cassidy said, and they headed down that way. She wasn't sure what her plan was. But she had put on makeup and done something with her hair for the night, so she might as well show up.

They went to the bar and ordered two bottled waters, then found a table to stand at. Getting her bearings in the loud nightclub, she spotted Jesse on the dancefloor twirling the lovely Hannah who fell clumsily into his arms, stumbling a bit from either too much drink or the appearance of it.

Rather than getting uptight about Jesse dancing with another woman, Cassidy just felt silly. What had she been thinking, anyway? Cassidy was shined up for the night with hair and makeup and a pretty kick-ass outfit, she didn't mind admitting, but she was no match for the young Hannah. "Well, that does it for me," she said, turning toward the door.

"Just, hang on," Sebastian said. "I know this looks bad, but watch his body language. He's putting her off. Look, right there." Hannah plunged into him again and looked up at him with *kiss me* eyes like

Cassidy had never seen. She had to hand it to the young woman. She knew how to flirt. Jesse stood up tall and glanced around the room, landing his gaze on the door. Sebastian backhanded Cassidy. "Oh my God, look. He's watching the door for you."

"Oh, please," Cassidy said, hoping it was true.

"He is, look at him."

Hannah whispered something in his ear with a grin on her face. Cassidy tried to control the wave of unease going through her stomach, but there was no hope. Jesse scratched his forehead, sort of squinting with one eye, saying something to her with a little shake of his head.

Sebastian covered his heart. "Oh Christ this is painful to watch. He totally just rejected her."

He reached down and hugged her as her grin morphed into humiliation. Sebastian put his fingers to his temple. "I've got to look away. This is brutal."

"He looks like he's being kind," Cassidy said, ashamed of how relieved she felt.

"That's what's so brutal. How horrible to be rejected by a guy who's being nice to you. If he was being a jerk she could hate him." As the two broke apart, Hannah glanced around the room looking a little lost, and then finally went to a table where she pulled a phone out of her purse and flipped through it. Cassidy imagined how she would feel if this same thing happened to her niece Seanna, and her heart went out to the girl.

"Oh, look. He's spotted you."

Cassidy drew her attention from Hannah and found Jesse, who was walking off the dance floor. He held up a hand in a wave, and she smiled at him.

"Okay, I believe my work here is done." Sebastian patted her twice on the shoulder. "Good night, Cinderella."

Jesse approached, all cleaned up and shaved wearing a black V-neck T-shirt with a silver chain around his neck, a pair of jeans that were designed for his body, and some black boots that made Cassidy's heart twist. She blew out a calming breath, wishing she wouldn't give this man the power to make her feel this way.

"Wow," he said. "You look really good."

She cocked her head to one side, taking in the view. "I'm not the only one."

His smile widened. "Did you have fun at the bachelorette thing?"

"Oh, yes. Marigold made sure Shayla was treated like a bachelorette princess."

"Nice...I think."

Cassidy shrugged.

"Did you guys get her a stripper?"

"No. Why? Did Chase have one?"

Jesse chuckled. "No, these guys don't strike me as the stripper sort. And isn't Bo the bride's brother?"

"Oh yes. That wouldn't have gone over well, I suppose. Have you guys been here all night?"

"We just got here about half an hour ago. We went to dinner down the street at an Asian restaurant. It was good. I don't really eat out like that much. I'm always at the bar on Friday and Saturday nights."

"I don't either, believe me. If it weren't for frozen dinners I'd starve to death." They both glanced around, Cassidy's gaze landing on their group across the way. Megan and Hannah sat at a table with Blake and Bo. "I hope I didn't interrupt your evening," Cassidy said.

Jesse furrowed his brow at her and then dropped his posture in realization. "You saw me dancing with Hannah."

Cassidy held up both hands. "She's lovely. Very kind young woman."

"I told her I was into someone else and I didn't want to mess that up."

Cassidy let out a sigh, shaking her head. "You didn't need to do that."

"I didn't need to, but I wanted to."

She met his gaze. "I just don't get that, Jesse. Hannah's a beautiful girl. Seanna says she's a really hard-worker. Very sharp. She's gracious and polite. She's everything I would think a guy like you would look for. Why wouldn't you want to give her a chance?"

"Man, I've been rejected before but never with that kind of sales pitch."

She smiled, shaking her head. "I'm not rejecting you. I'm just trying to understand you."

He pinched her hip. "Well stop."

She glanced over to the spot where their whole group was sitting and took a step away from Jesse, being led by pure instinct.

"Wow," he said. "You are embarrassed of me."

"I'm not," she said, hoping it wasn't a lie, but cringing as Blake caught sight of her and Jesse with a curious look on his face.

"I think I'm just gonna go to bed," she said.

He glanced at the time on his phone. "At ten-thirty?"

She tossed up both hands. "What can I say? I'm old."

"You can keep trying to convince me of that, but I'll never buy it."

She ran her hand across her forehead, heat flowing up through her chest. "I'll see you tomorrow, okay?"

"Okay," he said, and she willed her feet to walk away from him.

She headed upstairs and opened the door to her room, the emptiness of it swallowing her whole. She brushed her teeth, scrubbed off her makeup, changed into her favorite tank and cotton shorts, and got into bed. Flipping channels on the television couldn't have been a more futile exercise.

After catching up on emails and shared articles she'd been banking in her phone, she laid back and stared at the ceiling. Why could she not get Jesse off her mind? All she was picturing was him downstairs in that bar hooked back up with Hannah or a cast of new characters she hadn't even dreamed up yet. This wasn't her life. In her life pre-Jesse, she spent her nights with a glass of wine and whatever was on A&E. She didn't even have to see a series or even an episode from the beginning because she didn't really care. It was just a tool to numb her mind for the moment. But all she could picture in her brain was Jesse's gorgeous face.

She stilled as she heard a door from the hallway open and shut. She was almost positive that was him. Silence for a bit, then water running. A single squeak of the bed, and then more silence. The idea of him sharing the wall with her filled her with a fluttering anxiety. She was almost powerless against his draw, and he wasn't even doing anything to pull her in at the moment.

She inhaled a deep breath and then sat on the side of her bed. Surely she wasn't really thinking of knocking on that door. That would bring him into her room, and into her bed. God, the idea of his delicious mouth on hers fed her soul like sunlight.

She was out of her mind. Temporarily insane, that's what she'd claim. All she needed to do was tuck back into bed and give herself a quick orgasm, and then she'd be fine. That was the plan. Now, she just needed to stick to it.

Chapter Twelve

Jesse lay on his bed with nothing on but his boxers thinking about who was lying right behind him. What was it going to take to make this woman interested in him? He could knock on her door. She definitely seemed attracted to his body. But that wasn't what he wanted her to be interested in. He wanted her to connect with him. He wanted to talk about what she read and what made her get up in the morning other than the sheer need to make a living. He wanted to know what she'd done with the past couple of decades. What had her life been like? Where did she want it to lead? Was she planning on staying in Seaside and baking muffins, or was she banking money for something bigger one day? Was Jamaica her ultimate goal? What was holding her back? He had more questions than he could even formulate in his brain.

All he had to do was knock on that door, see if

she'd let him in when nobody was around to see them. He understood that she was embarrassed of him. He wasn't even sure he could argue that point. He was a twenty-nine-year-old bartender. She was a sophisticated woman used to dating guys her age or older. His ego was bruised, of course, but he couldn't wallow in that shit. He wanted her. He just needed to figure out how to make her proud to be on his arm.

He stood and found a T-shirt to put on. He started digging through his suitcase for a pair of shorts, but froze when a knock sounded at his door...the connecting one. He stood and glanced around like he was caught. She was coming for him. This was a pleasant turn of events. For all she knew he was in bed, so he wasn't going to put on a pair of shorts. He considered taking off his T-shirt and just answering the door in his boxers, but that was cheating. He wanted her to want to be with him without his bare chest as a dangling carrot.

He settled on boxers with the T-shirt and opened the door to find her standing there in a tank top with no bra and the sexiest little sleep shorts he'd ever seen. He gripped the side of the door, flexing his arm muscles. He had to cheat a little because she damn sure had. "What's up?" he said, his voice low after being quiet for a while and the long day and night getting to him.

"I'm just having a really hard time sleeping, so I thought I'd invite some company over."

He lifted his eyebrows. "Me?" He peered into her hotel room. "Do you think anyone will see me in here?"

She grabbed his hand. "Just get in here." Once she

got him into her room, she just stood there biting her thumbnail.

He lifted an eyebrow. "Did you not think this far?"

She let out an exhausted sigh, but her face was so red he could probably melt an ice cube on it. The idea of an ice cube melting on her skin made him twitch down below.

She offered an arm toward her king-sized bed. "Would you like to sit with me here and watch a movie?"

"Sure," he said. "I think there's popcorn in our gift baskets. Did you go through yours yet?"

"Oh my gosh. How did I forget about that thing?" She went over to the desk where it was sitting and pulled the string on it.

"You haven't even gone through it yet? You've got willpower."

"I just wasn't thinking about it." She brought it over to the bed and dumped it out. "Oh, wow. Movie boxes of candy. This is awesome."

"Give me those M&M's," he said.

She held the box to her chest. "Over my dead body."

He grabbed another box. "Fine. I'll just have to eat your cherries."

Her eyes got wide and then she looked down at the box in his hand. "Are those sour cherries?"

"I should have known you'd like these. Sour beer. Sour cherries. Makes sense."

She pulled out the bottle of wine. "Oh, I love this brand. And the best part is it's a twist off."

"Fire it up." He hopped off the bed and found a

couple of plastic cups. "I will say though that we have a habit of opening up bottles of wine and then not drinking them."

She gave him a look. "One time does not a habit make. Give me those cups."

She opened the bottle and then poured wine into the two cups he was holding out for her. She set the bottle down and he handed her the cup. "Cheers."

"To what?"

"To Chase wanting to spend his every last dime on us this weekend."

She touched her cup to his. "Here, here." After taking a sip, she said, "Although, I'm sure he's got a little to spare."

He swallowed the wine which was not at all shabby. "I'm sure he does." He held out his hand. "Give me some of your cherries."

She poured some into his hand. "You haven't had your fill of those yet?" she asked, trying to hold back her smile.

"Of your cherries? Are you kidding me? I live for your cherries."

She smiled, shaking her head at him. He loved it when she did that. It meant he'd stumped her, and each time she didn't take the opportunity to blow him off told him he was another step closer to landing her.

She read his T-shirt. "Who's that? A band?"

"Yeah, they played in the bar one night. I got into them for a while."

"What kind of music do you listen to?"

"I like indie rock. Mainstream alt rock is fun sometimes as long as it doesn't go too pop. It's been trying to do that lately. What about you?"

She exhaled, thinking. "I guess I'm a cliché of my generation. I listen some to stuff like Elle King and Young the Giant, The Revivalists, but I always find my way back to my old standards."

"What are those?" he asked.

She lay back against the many pillows this resort provided per bed, balancing her wine cup on her thigh. "Tori Amos, 10,000 Maniacs, Aimee Mann, oh, and my heart belongs to Liz Phair."

"I'm not sure if I can compete with her. She's damn hot."

She looked at him curiously. "You know Liz Phair?"

"I can remember a CD cover of hers from when I was a teenager. She had her legs spread out in front of her and she was holding this guitar between them. God, I must have whacked off to that a thousand times."

"Whose CD was it?"

"My sister's probably. I stole it though as soon as I laid eyes on it."

"Did you ever listen to it?"

"Didn't need to. It was serving its purpose. I was seventeen."

She hid her eyes. "God. I was at least your age now when that came out, probably older. How old's your sister?"

"She's six years older. She was back home from college during that time period."

"What's she like?"

"Nothing like me, that's for sure. She doesn't approve of my lifestyle."

She narrowed her gaze. "What kind of lifestyle is

that?"

"Bar life. I live above my shop. She lives in the suburbs."

"Does she have a family?"

He nodded. "Three kids and a husband."

"Do you like her husband?"

He shrugged. "He's fine. Buttoned-up. We talk about sports when I'm there, which is a stretch because I'm not into sports."

"So how do you talk about them then?"

He set his wine cup down and poured some M&M's into his hand. "I watch *SportsCenter* for a week before I go up there for Christmas."

She smiled. "Do they live in Louisville?"

"Yep, a suburb of it called Indian Hills."

She nodded. "Is she a stay-at-home mom?"

"Oh, yeah."

"Why do you say it like that?"

"Because she treats me like her fourth kid. Why the hell do you think I moved away?"

"Are you close with her kids?"

Jesse's heart panged a little. "I guess I should be. It's tough though because I only see them at Christmastime. You know what it's like owning your own business where we do. We're only slow in the winter. It's not like I can leave and go on vacation in the summer."

"I get it." Her expression turned thoughtful and she smiled a little.

"What?"

"Do you ever wonder if people like us start businesses in faraway cities to avoid our families?"

He rolled over onto his back, threading his fingers

together over his stomach. "I'll cop to that."

"Do you have any other siblings?"

His stomach soured. "A brother. Older."

"Ah, you're the baby."

He rolled his eyes.

"That's okay." She tugged at his T-shirt. "I'm the baby, too. Maybe we have more in common than I realized."

"Maybe we do," he said, looking at the television without a clue what was on.

"So what's he like?"

"Who?" he asked, a delay tactic.

"Your brother," she said, and then tossed back some candy.

He glanced around. "Where's the remote? Aren't we about to watch a movie?"

She handed it to him, eyeing him. No, he was not going to talk about his brother. Not tonight.

He started flipping. "Did you have something specific in mind?"

"I guess I should say yes," she said.

He smiled at the television, stopping on the only channel that wasn't running a commercial. It was something that looked like it'd been filmed in the sixties or seventies. He'd gotten interested in that old stuff ever since he and Gracie lost the remote that one day and got stuck watching a marathon of *The Love Boat*. That had taken them into a stint with *Fantasy Island*, and then *Charlie's Angels*. The acting on all the shows was so bad it made them good. "What's this?" he asked, not expecting an answer.

"Oh, God," she said. "Keeping going."

The fact that she wanted him to turn it just made

it more interesting. "Do you know what this is?"

"Mmm hmm. Can I please see the remote?"

He grinned over at her. She was blushing again. "Seriously, what is it?"

She started grabbing for the remote, so he held it out of her reach, trying to watch the show all at once. "What is this? A story about a boy and his grandma?"

She sat back on the bed. "No, not quite."

Now that he wasn't trying to fend her off, he could figure out where the info button was and see for himself. He hit it. "*Harold and Maude*," he read aloud.

Cassidy held both arms out, her wine cup still in her hand, and glanced up at the ceiling. "Are you freaking kidding me?"

"What?" he asked through a chuckle. "What's wrong with this movie?"

She gave an exhausted sigh and then pointed with her wine cup. "They're not grandmother and grandson. They're…romantic."

His mouth dropped open. "Are you fucking serious?"

"I'm dead serious. It's a cult classic. You've never heard of it?"

"No, but we're definitely watching it. When did it start?"

"Not too long ago," she said, resigned.

He met her gaze. "We don't have to."

"No, it's actually a really good movie. I had the luxury of watching it without having a clue what it was. I took all these cinema studies classes in college which made me really interested in all sorts of films. So I was home from college one weekend on a

Saturday afternoon, and this movie came on. I was totally sucked in and clueless about the plot, and so as they grew closer it was extra fascinating to me."

"Oh man. I wish I didn't know now."

"I'm sorry. Now I feel like I ruined it for you."

"Nah. I'm not like that. I can come in the middle of a movie or a TV show and be just fine."

She looked at him curiously. "I can, too."

He shrugged. "It's a special skill. We should be able to list it on our resumes."

"Lord knows mine needs work."

He turned toward her. "I know bakery owner. Fill me in on the rest."

She inhaled a deep breath, looking off into space. "God, the whole ugly thing?"

"Start with high school. What was your first job?"

She smiled. "I worked at a frozen yogurt shop."

"I'm sensing a theme here."

"I know. I swear I'm not addicted to sweets. I honestly could take them or leave them." She held up the M&M box. "Except for these, of course. What was your first job?"

"Construction. My buddy's dad had a company so he and I both worked for it."

"Ah, working guy." She took his hand and inspected it. "Yeah, you definitely look like you've worked with your hands." She grinned. "Probably way more than I care to know about."

She went to pull away, but he took a look at her long, slender hand, a tiny tremble in it. He met her gaze, curiously. What was she nervous about?

"I've definitely worked with my hands over the years," she said. "Proof is in the pudding."

Her hands were marked with a few scars and imperfections. "These look like hands that have enjoyed life."

She laughed. "Very kind way of putting it."

He threaded his fingers through hers and they rested their hands between them which gave him a natural peace of sorts. "Did you ever work a desk job?" he asked.

"Oh, for about five minutes. I temped when I got out of college and was well on my way to corporate hell when I met this friend who had volunteered for the Peace Corps." She shrugged. "So I figured I'd give that a try."

"You were in the Peace Corps?" he asked, not sure why he was so incredulous. He guessed *admiring* was a better word.

"Yeah, I was, for about two years."

"Wow," he said, feeling wholly inadequate. "What did you do?"

"My focus was in health, mainly in HIV/AIDS education."

He winced, thinking about her asking him to wear two condoms that night on the beach. No fucking wonder. "Wow. I imagine you've seen a lot of stuff, doing that."

She nodded, staring down at the bed, seeming to drift off into another world. "It was a time when AIDS was a death sentence. I don't know how your generation feels about it, but mine was scared straight. Have you ever seen *Reality Bites*?"

He shook his head.

"Anyway, it's a different time now, at least for those who have access to medicine and healthcare.

Definitely not like that for everyone."

He nodded, the sins and carelessness of his past creeping up his spine.

"Have you ever had a scare?" she asked.

He appreciated her kind way of asking him if he had HIV or AIDS. "I guess I was pretty careless a few years back. I didn't test positive for HIV, but I did catch something." He winced.

To her credit, her expression remained impassive. "Something curable, I hope." She said it not in a judging way, but sincerely.

He pinched his temple. "Chlamydia."

"Well, it is a popular one, isn't it? Did you have to call all your exes and tell them?"

"That was fun. I called as many as I could, but…" He trailed of, too embarrassed to finish the sentence.

"You didn't remember them all?" she asked.

"I probably can remember all of them, I just didn't get all their information."

"But with Instagram and Snapchat and all that these days, surely?"

He shook his head. "I'm not on any of that."

"Really?"

He didn't want to explain why. "Not my thing. Anyway, it all freaked me the hell out. I've been careful ever since."

"Usually just takes one scare for that. You got lucky."

"You think I don't know that?"

"How often do you get tested now?"

"I try to remember to go every six months."

"When's the last time you went?"

He thought about it, wanting to give her an honest

answer. "I think it was last summer. July maybe." He considered her. "What about you?"

"I get tested when I see my gynecologist for my yearly exam. I went when I got back from Jamaica."

"You've never had anything?"

"No, but it's only because I'm pretty much always careful. Like I said, I come from a different generation. We don't mess around with that. I know it feels better without a condom and all that, but our lives were at stake back then."

"I get it," he said, and then smiled. "So pure."

"Ha! Now that's funny." She looked at him thoughtfully. "So of all those girls who you passed through, were there any who stuck around for a while?"

He looked down at his hands. "Not especially."

"What about a high school sweetheart? Did you have one of those?"

"No," he said, truthfully. He hadn't met Lauren until college.

"So you've never had a long-term relationship?" she asked, not seeming to believe him.

He let out a resigned breath. He wasn't ready to do this. Not tonight. "I did, actually. In college."

"How long did that last?"

He shook his head at the ceiling, the pain from that time period gut-punching him again. "Too damn long."

She waited him out, wordlessly, and as much as it pained him, he figured now was as good a time as any.

"Four and a half years through college, and then two and a half after we graduated."

"Wow. That sounds really serious. Were you planning on getting married?"

"We'd mutually decided to wait to get engaged. She was in law school and I was working for her father."

"Doing what?"

"Accounting."

She sat up. "Are you serious?"

He nodded, glancing over to see the shock on her face. He forced a smile. "Don't look too surprised."

"I shouldn't be. You do own your own successful business. It's just that I can't imagine you in a million years working in accounting. Did you wear a suit?"

"On occasion. But typically the uniform was khakis and a polo."

She giggled. "I'm sorry. But I just can't picture that. Did you have the tattoos then?"

"No, I didn't get those till after. Lauren hated tattoos." It was so weird saying her name. He hadn't said it in years.

"So how did you go from that life to the one you have now?"

He scratched his head, his heart clenching from just having to say the words. Nobody in his current life knew anything about what had happened except for Dane, and he, of course, never mentioned her. He knew not to.

"Her parents had a big party for her when she graduated law school. We were all there—her family, my family, all our friends. My brother showed up, which I didn't think a lot about at first, because he'd known Lauren as long as I had. We all went to UK together. I'd noticed Lauren had been

123

missing for a while, so I went inside to find her, and I did, in her room."

She held her hand over her heart. "Oh no."

"They weren't in bed together. I think I may have preferred it if they had been. Instead, they were sitting on the bed, and she was crying. He had her cradled to him, kissing the top of her head." A wave of embarrassment flowed through his body. "Like the biggest moron on the planet, I went to her and kneeled down in front of her, my hands on her knees. I asked her what had happened. Was it one of her parents? Was someone sick?" He shook his head, the memory so vividly wicked and fresh. "She was sitting there cuddled up to my brother, and my first thought was to comfort her. Have you ever heard of a bigger moron?"

"I think that makes you kind and compassionate."

His thoughts went dark and murderous. "He did the talking for them. They'd fallen in love. They hadn't meant to hurt me. It'd never been the right time to tell me. They didn't want to do anything to derail her plans of graduating law school, so they'd kept it a secret. They'd been fucking one another for years. I couldn't get them to tell me how long it'd been going on, but I'm pretty sure I can pinpoint it back to my junior year of college. She broke up with me for a few weeks and then she came back to my apartment bawling one night, begging me to take her back. She'd made a huge mistake. She would never do it again. I suspected she'd slept with someone, but I didn't care. Not enough. I wanted her back. That was all I knew. My brother was still in Lexington at the time, working out an internship. Her coming back to me lined up with him going home after the internship was over. I knew it at the time, but I refused to believe it."

Cassidy reached for his thigh, laying her hand on it and running her thumb back and forth, calming his darkened mind.

"So how long did they stay together afterward?"

He exhaled a deep breath. "They're still fucking together."

"Oh my God, Jesse. I'm so sorry."

He shrugged.

"This might be a strange question, but you said you worked for her dad. Was he grooming you for big things at his company, or…"

"Oh yeah. That was the plan. Her dad and I were close. We played golf at least once a week. I was a part of their family. He kept me really close at work. I started near the bottom, but he pulled me into all kinds of meetings I didn't belong in. 'Watch and learn,' he'd always tell me. I'd eat lunch in his office and he'd run ideas and proposals by me. He valued me and I worked my ass off to show him I was worthy of his time and all he was prepping me for."

"What did he think when this all happened?"

"He was stunned. Livid. He'd invested three years in me and promoted me a couple of times. He had too many bourbons one night and told me the company would be ours one day, mine and Lauren's."

"Wow. This must have been a shock to him."

"Oh yeah."

"So did your brother step into your shoes at the company, too?"

"He tried. Bill, her dad, told me he worked there

four months and then bailed for another job. His major was finance, but he always hated it."

"You stayed in touch with her dad?"

"Yeah. He still calls me about once every six or eight months. Asks about the bar. Asks if I'm seeing anyone. He knows not to say much about Lauren, but I swear I think he's gauging me to see if I'd consider coming back. I don't think he's accepted the fact that his plan went to shit."

"The two of you must have had some kind of connection for him to continue keeping in touch."

He hesitated before he said his next words. Only Dane knew the truth. Others suspected, but nobody else knew for sure. "He's probably checking in to make sure his money is still going to good use. When I gave him my notice, officially, he paid me a year's worth of severance, lump sum. My salary was already inflated as it was, so I'd banked plenty already. I thanked him, took the money and drove south."

She huffed a laugh. "Good for you."

He turned to face her. "You don't think less of me for taking his money?"

"Are you kidding me? Why wouldn't you? I'd have taken it."

"You'd have given it to charity, too."

"Not necessarily. The money I used to open Seaside Sweets wasn't totally pure."

"How'd you get that money?"

"A sort of ex of mine died and left me some money. He was a man I dated on-and-off for several years during my thirties, someone I'd met on a volunteer trip. We had very different lives. He was a corporate type who lived in Pittsburgh. I was never going to live in Pittsburgh," she said with a smile. "But I did enjoy him. I could have loved him if I'd allowed myself to. But I'd known better."

"You can do that? Just shut off your heart like that?"

She cut her eyes at him. "I like to act like I can."

His heart swelled with this hint of vulnerability she showed him. "What were you doing before you got that money?" he asked.

"I was working in elderly care. My mom had died and she'd been in a rehab center at the time, which was a glamorous way to say nursing home. The people who worked there were hit or miss, but this one woman was so dedicated to her patients. I was going to be this woman. I was going to sign up and dedicate my life to these elderly people in need." She shook her head. "Needless to say, I didn't stack up. I wanted to be as selfless as my mentor was, but I wasn't even close. It was the hardest work I've ever done. I thought I would get used to the smell but I didn't. It was back-breaking work, holding up the dead weight of a person over the toilet or trying to move them up on a bed. I'd promised myself I'd do it for a year, and I kept that promise, but when I got that money a few months in, it was like a guarantee of parole." She met his gaze, a shameful look on her face. "I sound awful."

"I think that's a whole lot more time than most people give."

She waved him off. "I'm no humanitarian. I give it a college try every once in a while, but I use Seaside Sweets as my crutch. 'I'm sorry I'll have to skip this trip. I've got the shop.' I can only imagine the eye rolls on the other end of the phone when they call." She looked at him abruptly. "God, listen to me. I don't know what's gotten into me."

"It's called opening up to someone. Haven't done it in a while?"

She smiled at him, a true, genuine smile that meant something. He had no idea what, but something was going on between them. "I guess I have not." She peered over him at the end table. "You're not drinking your wine."

"I feel buzzed enough just lying here with you."

"Yeah, because talk of nursing home work will really do that to you."

"Getting to know you does that to me."

She took a sip of her wine through a little smile— his reward for putting himself out there. She held the cup between them. "So have you and your brother reconciled?"

He looked up at the ceiling. "We don't speak."

"What do you do about the holidays?"

"I only go for Christmas. My sister has it at her house. Lauren's family does their big get-together on Christmas Eve, so that's when I go to my sister's house. They come over for Christmas Day and I'm headed back here by then."

"So you travel up there for one day?"

"It's what I've done for the past few years now."

"Do they have kids?"

His heart stung. "They've got a baby."

She put her hand to her mouth and messed with her chin.

"What?" he asked, feeling defensive.

"I just hate that you deal with this. It sounds like a miserable way to live."

"I'm doing fine," he said, totally not fine.

"What does your sister say about it all?"

He shook his head, his anger rising again. "She has very specific opinions, all of which involve me being a bigger person than I am and reaching out to him to make up."

"Surely she was outraged at the time, though."

"Oh, not as much as you'd think. Turns out she'd known for years. She'd caught them huddling close at a family event where apparently I was off being clueless somewhere. She swears she begged him to come clean, but that he swore it was over and that telling me would just hurt me. They'd mutually decided how to handle me. Fuck them," he said, his fury getting the better of him.

She set her wine cup down on the table next to her, and then reached over and put her hand on his chest where his heart was and rubbed gently back and forth, calming him. She moved closer to him and trailed kisses on his forehead as if she was trying to take away his pain. It might just be temporary, but hell if it wasn't working. She kissed around his face and down to his mouth. His hand drew to cup the back of her neck, and she draped herself over him, a warmth like he'd never known filling him from top to bottom.

"I wasn't going to do this," he whispered, touching her cheeks with the tips of his fingers as her hair fell around his neck and onto his chest.

"What are you doing?" she asked between kisses.

"I was gonna be cocky and make you want me all

night."

She pulled back from him. "I think that was going to happen no matter what."

She tugged his shirt up his torso, and he lifted up so she could take it off of him. Laser-focused on him, she admired his chest like a fine art sculpture, smoothing her hands over his shoulders and then down his torso. "You're so beautiful, it makes me feel guilty. No one woman should be this lucky."

His ego could indulge in those words for days. Moving down his body, she must have kissed every inch of his torso while her hands explored his waist, her fingers hooking inside the waistband of his boxers.

He'd promised himself he would not sleep with her tonight. Instead, he was going to show her that this wasn't just a fling for him. He wanted this to be about more than sex for her, and the way to do that was to leave her curious and wanting. But here she was traveling down his legs, his cock as hard as steel in her hand. She stroked his length slowly, making him nuts with want.

She took him into her mouth, and his eyes closed as he relaxed into her slow, deliberate motions up and down his length. Fuck that felt good. He let all the negative thoughts and the pain of the past drift away as he thought of nothing but the sensations flowing through him thanks to her. He gripped the bedding as she worked magic on him, bringing him to the brink faster than he could control. He was barely aware of himself saying her name as the sensations rose, and he nudged her away, grabbing his cock, emptying himself onto his stomach.

"Fuck," he said, breathlessly as he let go of himself, his arms falling onto the pillow beside his head, his eyes closed as he caught his breath.

He was aware of her leaning over him and pulling a few tissues out of the box on the nightstand next to him. He opened his eyes and she handed them to him. "That was considerate of you," she said.

"It was the least I could do." He stood and dropped his boxers to the floor while he went to the bathroom to clean up. Admittedly, he'd have used the tissue with anybody else and just tossed it away on the floor. But he wanted to be on his best behavior for her.

When he returned, he found her lying on her side, her elbow propping herself up, head in her hand, her long legs stretched out on the bed. She looked a good as Gisele or any other supermodel he'd ever seen. "It's not fair for one person to be so goddamned sexy."

She smiled at him. "You can stop trying. I think you've already got the best of me tonight."

He shoved the candy boxes and the gift basket onto the floor and then slid onto her. "I haven't even gotten started."

He kissed her, their tongues meeting in their now familiar way. He could do nothing but kiss her the rest of the night and be satisfied, but if he was going to make sure she kept coming back to him, he needed to do better than that.

He slid his hands up her tank top and over her breasts, which couldn't have fit into his hands better if they tried. They were absolute perfection, her breasts, just in proportion to her body. He lifted her shirt and took one of her hard nipples into his mouth. She slid her hands under her head, opening her whole body to him. He trailed kisses down her belly and then curled his fingers into the waistband of her shorts. She looked so good in them it was almost a shame to take them off...almost. He pulled them down her legs, discarding them onto the bed, and then slid his hands up her calves, over her knees, and then up her thighs, his thumbs toying with her inner thighs. He hadn't had the fortune of seeing her naked when they were on the beach, but it'd definitely been worth the wait. He parted her thighs, watching her close her eyes, her brow furrowed in anticipation. God he loved that he could make her look like that. She sucked in a little breath as he slid a finger inside of her, playing around until he found the spot that made her sing, her facial expression giving away all the secrets. He kept that up as he found her clit and watched her relax into his tongue, his cock going instantly hard as he got a taste of her.

She lifted up off the bed, taking him with her, and it was all he could do to keep from beaming with pride at what he could do to her. She froze as she held her breath and then let out a gasp as she collapsed down on the bed. He kissed his way back up to her stomach.

"Condom," she said, eyes still closed, pointing at the nightstand.

He grinned as he pulled open the drawer. "One or two?"

"One," she said, and he took it as a step closer to her. He'd broken through the stranger wall to one-condom status. Baby steps.

He suited up and then positioned himself above her. "You ready for me now, baby?" he asked.

She nodded, a crooked little smile on her lips that he could lick off. But he had other things to tend to.

He pushed into her wet warmth, the absence of the extra condom making a huge difference. He realized this was the second time they'd done this with her shirt on. They'd have to remedy that next time.

It wasn't going to take him long, unfortunately. With all the other random hookups, he could keep up the motion all night if he'd wanted to. But with her, there was something other than a primal need to fuck at play. Emotions were affecting his staying power. He could try to wish them away, but they were what was making this moment with her so superb.

"I'm not gonna last long," he admitted.

She put her hands around his waist. "Go whenever you're ready, gorgeous."

Just a few more thrusts and he lost his senses again. He collapsed on top of her, nudging into the crook of her neck, never wanting their bodies to separate again.

She rubbed her hand up and down his back in a soothing motion, and he swore he could sleep for three days exactly like that.

He lifted up and hovered over her, keeping his emotions in check. His feelings for her had skyrocketed after this one evening, but she could not know any of that. "Did I ruin anything for you? I mean, could you go again if I—"

"I'm still coming down off my high from the one a few minutes ago."

He nodded and kissed her, and then rolled off of

her and headed to the bathroom. After he washed his hands, he caught a glimpse of himself in the mirror. He pointed at himself. "Get control, asshole," he said, and then headed back to the bed.

When he returned, she had those cute little shorts back on, unfortunately, and her eyes were closed, but she didn't seem like she was asleep yet. He slid into bed beside her, wondering how she liked to sleep. She was an independent woman who'd been single for decades. Surely she wasn't into snuggling.

Eyes still closed, she scooted toward him and draped herself over him, her chest falling into a rhythmic pattern with his. He closed his eyes, drinking her in, this moment surpassing any other to date.

Chapter Thirteen

Indulging in a spa day had never seemed practical nor desirable for Cassidy, but she didn't mind saying she was luxuriating in it today as the masseuse rubbed her left foot. She was getting spoiled rotten this weekend. Between Chase treating them all to the best food, wine, and spas money could buy, Jesse had been feeding her senses and her soul.

She'd awoken to find him gone, but a note on his pillow said to be sure and miss him tons today. Any other millennial would have sent a text, but the fact that he cared enough to leave a note just gave her one more reason to fall for him.

And she was clear on that now. She was falling for him. Her feet were dug into the slide, but gravity was pulling her to him. It almost seemed like the more she resisted him, the more significant her feelings grew.

What a difference a night could make. She'd

uncovered so much about him. All this time, she'd been thinking he was a heartless player, but now she understood his struggle. Cassidy tried to put herself in his shoes, imagining her own sister having slept with Cassidy's significant other for years without her knowing. The idea of it all was so unimaginable. She'd sworn she wasn't going to start up anything physical between them, but he was so vulnerable lying there with all that pent-up anger and resentment. She couldn't help wanting to lighten his load and redirect his focus for the moment.

Oh the sex, holy mother of God. She could hold his rock hard cock in her hand from now till eternity and not get enough of it. Blowjobs had become a chore for her—a means to an end. She'd spent countless hours in the past several years going down on older men who couldn't get it up. She'd labor, her jaw muscles sore just to produce a partial erection which, once inside her, she couldn't even feel. The idea of going down on a man for pure pleasure, not only his but her own, hadn't occurred to her in years...until last night.

Just her kisses on his chest made him rock hard for her. She knew men that age could get erections from a change in the wind, but she couldn't help a sense of pride at the idea that she could give Jesse that kind of pleasure. She wanted to do it again. She wanted to do it right then.

The masseuse let her know she was finished and told her to come out when she was ready. Cassidy's only motivation for ever moving from that spot was talking to Jesse. God, she was getting this bad for him.

She ran into Shayla and Maya in the waiting room and told them she was going to head up to get ready. She showered and shaved her legs, primping way too long. But she couldn't help wanting to look good for him.

As she passed Jesse's room, she could hear the shower running from the hallway. God, just the idea of him there made her chest heat up. She couldn't believe the effect he was having on her.

The girls all met up in the bar at the hotel where they were drinking martinis. Shayla handed her one. "It's a cucumber martini. The bartender recommended it."

"Thank you," Cassidy said, taking a sip and then held it up to the bartender. "Delicious."

He smiled at her and then went back to work.

She glanced around. "The guys are on their way?"

"Yep, their fishing trip ran long. They're all getting ready."

Seanna grabbed Shayla to ask her a question, and Sebastian sidled up to Cassidy. "Well? How did last night go?"

Cassidy just smiled down at her drink.

"Oh God. That good?"

She nodded at him. "Be quiet though. I don't want to make a big deal out of it."

"Why? It sounds like an amazing deal. He's the nicest guy. I sat with him this morning at breakfast."

She blinked. "You did?"

"Yeah, the guys all met down here early for breakfast before the boat trip. You do know I'm a guy, right?"

She gave him a look. "You were at the spa with

us today."

"I know, but I get included on both text chats, the guys and the girls."

"Well, don't you seem special."

"He's so great, Cassidy. He's not your typical straight guy. I can actually talk with him. I asked him if he read, and we spent the next half hour passing book recs back and forth."

She nudged him. "I'm jealous. I haven't even gotten a chance to talk to him about books yet."

"He reads for at least an hour before bed every night. Just imagine him lying in bed, shirtless with a book. Can you stand it?"

"How do you know he sleeps shirtless?"

"This is my fantasy. He can be wearing whatever I want." His eyebrows went up. "Get your act together because he's read some serious lit."

"Noted," she said, realizing she may have to step it up if they became a couple. Then she immediately felt silly for her assumption.

Chase and Bo came in and the bartender got to work on more drinks. They all chatted as the men filed in one by one until finally Chase looked around. "Who are we missing?"

"Jesse's on his way down," Dane said, giving Cassidy ridiculous butterflies. She hadn't seen him since she'd fallen asleep on his chest last night.

"Cool." He turned to the bartender, holding up his drink. "One more of these then we'll be out of your hair."

Jesse walked into the bar wearing a pair of fitted black pants and a tan shirt with black cuffs and trim, looking like a trillion bucks.

"There he is!" Chase said with a big smile. No doubt Jesse had won Chase over by this point. "Bartender's working on your drink now."

"Cool," Jesse said with a nod. "Thanks."

He met Cassidy's gaze with a tempered smile, glancing around at the others there like he wasn't sure how he should approach her.

The idea of hiding her attraction to him now seemed ludicrous and damn near impossible. They'd taken a step last night. She wasn't sure where that step was going to lead them, but she understood now that pretending like nothing was happening here was no longer an option.

She stepped up to him and slid her arm around his waist. "Hey," she said.

His smile grew. "Hey."

"I followed your instructions. I missed you tons today."

"Good, because I damn sure missed you."

She leaned in and planted a kiss on his lips, his arm snaking around her waist, pulling her toward him. When they finally broke apart, Chase was standing there holding a drink. "Should I get a fire hose instead?"

As they headed to their table, life went on all around them, conversations having nothing to do with them. Cassidy felt like the biggest narcissistic asshole for ever dreaming of being embarrassed of him. Yes, he was way younger than her. But Jesse was a nuanced man with so much more to him than his age or beautiful face, or pant-worthy body.

Neither Jesse nor Cassidy could decide if they

wanted the eggplant or the scallops, so they each got one and shared with the other, taking bites off each other's plates with little fork fights here and there. Cassidy tried so hard to pay attention to all the conversations around them, but she kept being drawn back to Jesse whether he was looking at her or engrossed in another conversation.

It'd been eons since she'd felt this fluttery feeling in her belly, this crush-like state from when she was a kid. She'd all but thought those days had passed for her. She enjoyed men like Todd and the others she dated, but none of them made her giddy like this. She wasn't sure if that was a good or a bad thing.

"So it's pool and darts after this, right? At that bar down the street?" Marigold asked.

"Yep. Pool and darts," Dane confirmed, eyeing Jesse. "But something tells me we aren't going to see the two of you there."

Cassidy met Jesse's gaze with raised eyebrows. "Umm…"

He squeezed her thigh under the table. "I think we might skip darts and pool."

Chase, who had hearing like a bat, turned toward them from Jesse's left. "Who's not coming to darts and pool?"

"Everyone's coming," Marigold said. "Just get back to your tiramisu."

He glared at Jesse and Cassidy. "It's these two isn't it? Aww, hell. If that's the case then you're excused."

"Should we take offense to that?" Jesse asked Cassidy.

Chase waved a big hand around the table. "All

these other assholes have been together a while. You two are brand new, right? You're in that phase where you can't get out of bed. I wouldn't dream of making you suffer through a dart game."

Cassidy's neck heated up, but she couldn't help a smile as she took her last bite of vanilla mousse dessert.

"That's good of you, man," Jesse said with a handshake.

"You're both excused. We'll see you down here at ten to head to the airport."

Jesse turned to Cassidy with a shrug, and she scooted her seat back, shameless. After a plethora of thank you's for the dinner and the weekend, they were off.

As soon as the elevator doors closed, Jesse was on her, arms around her waist, and then down to her ass, giving it a squeeze. He kissed her, and then pulled away with a grin. "You taste like sweet cream," he said.

"You taste like chocolate," she said. "Nice combo."

The elevator dinged and they headed straight to his room, the closest. He let them in and they stumbled as they pulled down pants and discarded shirts. He reached around her back and undid her bra, then pulled the straps down her arms. "Finally. I can't believe I haven't seen these yet," he said, cupping them.

"Haven't you seen enough boobs to last a lifetime?" she asked.

"I think I can die now that I've seen yours."

She giggled and dropped her head back as he took

her nipple into his mouth. "Mmm," she moaned, his mouth on her breast lighting her up down below.

He slid his hand into her panties and two fingers directly inside of her, making her gasp. "Damn, that's the hottest thing ever," he said. "You're so wet for me."

Cassidy never did well with sexy talk, but coming from him, she could get on board.

She gripped his blessedly hard cock. "And this is for me?" she asked.

"Hell, fucking yeah it is," he said, pushing her down on the bed.

He started to head between her legs, but her body was so in need of him inside it, she wasn't sure if she could take the torture. She nudged his head away. "Just get a condom already."

He smiled. "I can do that." He jumped up and grabbed a small bag out of his suitcase and pulled one out. Within seconds he was plunging into her there, sideways on the bed. She gripped his biceps as the pressure mounted, taking her to places she'd only dreamed about. God, if only they could remove that condom between them, she'd freaking lose her mind. But she couldn't go nuts here. She'd been so good for so long, teaching others to be safe. She had to stay strong and resigned.

She let out a groan as he pushed hard inside her, over and over, the friction making her lose control. She dug her fingertips into his shoulders and let herself go with a loud sound of carnal bliss, and he collapsed onto her, breathing into her neck. After a moment of rest, he kissed her neck and then pulled off of her, lying on his back. "Fuck, Cassidy. I can't get enough of you."

She smiled and let that sink in for her.

While he was in the bathroom, she pulled the sheet up her naked body, feeling a little bit too exposed. When he headed back for the bed, he said, "Are you cold?"

"Not really," she said.

He slid into bed next to her, underneath the sheet, and ran his hand up her belly and between her breasts. "I could touch you every minute of every day."

"I could let you."

He ran a single finger down the length of her torso, brushing by her clit, and then cupping her thigh. "I love every inch of your body."

She froze, his wording throwing her off a little, but he just continued playing with her. She had to relax into this…just let it be what it was going to be.

"You're the one with the amazing body." She pulled the sheet off his chest so she could look at it. "Tell me about all your tattoos," she said, running her fingers over his arm.

"They're not anything super-significant, not those. I got the first one as kind of a fuck-you to my buttoned-up life, and then I got another one just because I'd had a hard time deciding that day and wanted to go back for the second one. From there it became kind of a habit."

"Do you think you'll get more?"

"If I feel like it, but I've been done for a while now. You don't have any, do you?" he asked. "Hang on." He lifted the sheet and took a look at her backside. He ran a hand over her ass, and then gave it pat, which made her feel twenty years younger for some odd reason. "I didn't think so. You never wanted one?"

"I had a moment when I thought about it, but it passed."

He ran a finger over her chest. "You ought to get one here in red. *Jesse Kirby is hot.*"

"You wouldn't see that as a little psycho?"

"Hell no. I'd parade you around town in tank tops all the time so everyone could see it."

She considered him. "It really doesn't bother you, being seen with an older woman?"

"Not like it bothers you to be seen with a younger guy."

She deserved that. "I made progress tonight, didn't I?"

He smiled. "Yeah, you did. I wasn't sure what to do when I first saw you. I didn't want you to think I was blowing you off or anything, but I wasn't sure how open you would be with me."

She gave him a resigned smile. "I'm sorry I ever made you feel that way. It was my hang-up. It had absolutely nothing to do with you personally."

"Exactly what hang-up is it that you got over?"

She inhaled deeply, knowing she was on thin ice here. This was so new, whatever it was. He seemed all in but these situations were delicate. Cassidy would never forget the guy who had once pursued her hard. Flirting shamelessly for nights on the phone. The second she gave it back to him he made an excuse to get off the phone and she never heard from him again. Men liked the chase. She understood this.

"I just wasn't sure where this was going. I'm still not sure, but I think we may be in the same arena." She gauged him. Might as well get it out on the table. She was interested. She was letting him know that.

He took her hand and threaded his fingers through hers. "I'm not only in the arena, I got us a pair of box seats."

She smiled. "Dang, you put some coin down for those, didn't you?"

"Damn right I did. Cost me a week's salary."

She shook her head, giggling. Freaking giggling.

"God, you're sexy when you let yourself laugh."

"You think I hold back?"

"Oh, yeah. You're so nonchalant. Disinterested."

"Wow, that doesn't sound good."

"Not unkind, but unaffected."

"Sounds like I put on a good front," she said.

He ran a finger over her forehead and down her nose. "You better watch out. I'm busting through that front. I'm coming for you, lady."

She closed her eyes, smiling so wide. He covered her mouth with a kiss, and they fell right back into their rhythm, but this time, they just kept kissing. He pulled away, staying close. "You have no idea how good you make me feel."

Her heart filled to the brim when he said things like that. She'd seen this as an affair. A handful of nights of progressing passion that would eventually fizzle when a pretty girl walked into his bar. And that still might be their fate. Only time would tell them for sure, and as soon as they got away from this fantasy weekend she would find out exactly where they stood.

Chapter Fourteen

Upon their return from the fantasy weekend, Cassidy had sworn to herself that she would buckle down at work for the week and not fall into a romance-induced coma. Knowing that Jesse had a lot to catch up on from being out, she told herself that she wouldn't try to see him until Sunday when the shop was closed, and she started counting down the minutes. She even let Marigold deliver the cookies on Tuesday, but after a WTF text with a single-tear emoji, she'd sworn she'd make the Wednesday delivery.

As she walked into the bar, showered, hair done, and makeup on, a first for a workday for her, Jesse, snatched her up and twirled her around, barely giving her time to set the cookies down. She was thin, but she was a big girl. She was worried he'd hurt his back, but then she remembered his age and subsequent strength.

He set her down. "I can't believe I haven't seen you for a full forty-eight hours."

"Well, we left each other at about six o'clock on Monday, and it's eleven o'clock on Wednesday, so I think we're more like, forty-one hours."

"Forty-one too many," he said, kissing her like they weren't standing in the middle of a place of business.

"Ahem," Kelly, one of the servers, uttered as she passed with raised eyebrows.

He took Cassidy's hands. "Come upstairs with me."

She glanced around like there was someone there who would get them in trouble. "Really?"

"I'm gonna lose my mind if I don't have you right fucking now." He slid his hands over her hips and down to her ass.

She stepped back, smiling. "Okay." It wasn't like she hadn't prepared for this possibility. This was a young, very sexual man, and it'd been two days since they'd last made love…had sex.

He led her through the door that promised to squeal but did not, and up the stairs to a door that was not locked.

Just as they got through the doorway, he went for her at the same time his phone buzzed. He looked at it. "Fuck. Hang on. Can you not just handle it?" he asked as he typed. He waited for the response and then rolled his eyes. "Don't move. I'll be right back." He pointed at a door. "That one's mine. Go make yourself comfortable. Get naked." He went for the door and then came back to her and kissed her, threading his fingers through her hair. He pulled away. "I'll be right back."

He ran down the stairs, leaving Cassidy standing in his apartment a little dumbfounded. She wasn't sure what she had expected, but it looked exactly like a slightly upgraded college roommate type apartment. A decent leather sofa. A television that was definitely not the latest technology. A large plastic bowl that may have had cereal in it earlier that day, she hoped, on the coffee table. Tons of wires coming from the TV stand. A video game console. She felt like she could have handled anything but the video game console.

The sound of a door opening stunned her so epically that she gave a little shout, holding her hand over her heart. A very young girl stepped out of a room wearing nothing but thong underwear and a T-shirt that exposed her belly, stopping just below two ample breasts that were either fake or outstanding.

The girl scratched her head, her shirt lifting up to almost expose her nipple. "Hey. I thought I heard Jesse come back." She squinted at her. "You're not his sister are you?"

"Umm," Cassidy said, having trouble taking her eyes off the girl's exposed body. "No."

"Mmm," she grunted, and then headed to the kitchen and opened the refrigerator door. "Dammit. I've got to do a grocery order."

Cassidy wasn't sure she'd ever been stunned into submission, but that was exactly what was happening in that moment.

The girl turned back to her, setting a bowl on the counter. "I'm Gracie."

Cassidy wasn't sure if she should give this person

her name or not. But honestly, the girl didn't look interested in knowing it, which encouraged her to give it. "I'm Cassidy."

Gracie forced a smile. "Nice to meet you. Sorry I don't have anything to offer you."

"It's no problem. I'll tell you what. I'm just going to head out. It was lovely to meet you."

"Is Jesse not coming back?"

"No, I think he might be. I have a question, actually. Can I go out this back door? The one that exits to outside at the bottom of this staircase, or will that trigger an alarm?"

"No, that's totally how we come and go."

Cassidy smiled out of pure relief. "That's great. Thank you for your hospitality."

"No problem." Gracie looked her up and down. "Do you do barre?"

"Excuse me?"

"You're like, hot for an older lady. I want to look like you when I'm your age. What's your workout?"

"Umm," Cassidy said, utterly clueless. "I'm just gonna..." She trailed off as she opened the door.

"Bye," Gracie said, lifting her hand up high. Cassidy pushed through the door just before getting a glimpse of what had to have been her exposed nipple.

Cassidy ran down the stairs, begging the gods to let her get out the door before he came back in, but as soon as she pushed through the *out* door, she heard the other door open.

"Cassidy?" came Jesse's voice, which now full-on gave her the creeps. Picking up her step, she started a jog in the direction of her car. "Cassidy!" he yelled and, of course, caught up with her. "Hey, what's going on?"

Cassidy stopped, realizing running was futile at this point. He was in way better shape. She pinched the bridge of her nose. "Umm, I met Gracie."

He just stood there looking confused for a moment, and then understanding finally seemed to sink in. "Oh, fuck. Have I not mentioned her yet?"

She couldn't help a laugh. "No."

"She's my roommate. I forgot she was home. She's usually up and gone by now but she's on spring break."

"Spring break?" Cassidy asked. One of many questions she didn't want the answer to.

"She goes to community college in Niceville. They don't have class this week. I forgot all about that."

Cassidy scrunched up her face, trying to continue to make sense of this. "Does she typically walk around mostly naked?"

"Oh, fuck," he said, running his hand through his hair. "I'm so sorry, Cassidy. I swear, she and I are totally plutonic."

"Okay, I'd really like to believe that, but I want you to imagine that you've stepped into my home and found a very attractive man walking around in his underwear. What would your feeling about that be?"

He tossed up his hands. "I'd want to fucking kill him."

"Can you maybe understand that I have some questions? For one, why haven't you mentioned this?"

He held up a hand. "I swear to God, I wasn't trying to hide it. It just never came up. I don't see her that much at home anyway."

"At home?" she asked.

"She works at the bar. That's how we know one another."

Cassidy closed her eyes, letting that gem sink in. "Hang on. This woman works for you?"

"Yeah," he said, like that made perfect sense.

"And you see her walking around your house half naked on a daily basis?"

He shrugged. "Yeah, but it's just not a big deal."

She narrowed her gaze at him, understanding banging her upside the head. "Is it not a big deal because she's an ex of yours?"

His hesitation to answer the question made her want to vomit. "I wouldn't call her an ex, exactly."

She held up both hands like she was being arrested. "I think I've heard all I need to for the day." She turned and headed toward her car.

"Please don't run away from me. I really want a chance to explain this."

She shook her head at herself. What had she expected?

"Please, Cassidy. I can't let you walk away like this."

She stopped and turned toward him slowly. "I'm sorry. You can't *let* me?"

"This is spiraling out of control. Please, just listen to me for a minute. Can I have a minute?"

She let out an exhaustive sigh, wanting to get away, but somehow needing to hear the explanation for this nonsense.

"We used to sleep together on occasion. It was always just for fun. Neither of us ever took it seriously. She's not dating anyone right now, but she sees guys all the time, I swear."

"In your apartment?"

He shrugged. "Yeah."

She bit her lip, looking off at the ocean between the buildings. "I've made a huge mistake here," she said, her heart unable to believe the words it needed to hear.

"Look, I've never hidden my lifestyle from you. I told you I lived above my bar. You know I've slept around a lot. I'm honestly not sure why you're so shocked about this."

"Because," she said, her voice coming out way too loud. She gained control of herself. Nobody ever said anything good when they weren't rational. "Because there's a beautiful young girl at least half my age walking around half-naked in your apartment whom you have apparently slept with multiple times. Look, I'm easy, and open, and fluid, and whatever other term is en vogue right now, but as a human woman, that shit is not going to fly."

He dropped the tension in his shoulders, thinking as he stared at the sidewalk. He nodded like he was finally understanding. "I get it. Just let me figure something out, okay? I can't kick her out in the middle of the semester."

Her hand went to her forehead, rubbing it. She felt like the biggest heel on the planet. "You aren't going to kick her out now or ever. This is just a shock, okay? Can I have a minute to process it?"

He stared at her, fear in his eyes. "Okay," he said.

"That's fair enough. Can I come over tonight after you get off work?"

"Don't you need to be working then?"

"I'm always a floater in case someone doesn't show up. If everyone's there, they won't need me."

She let out a sigh. "Okay. Maybe, six?"

"I'll be there."

She nodded and then walked off toward the car, her brain bouncing around in her head. He was right. He had never lied about his lifestyle. It was all out there for her to view, chlamydia and all. She couldn't expect him to be all the things she wished he was no more than he could expect that of her. The worst part was she feared the emotion that was driving this train on her part was jealousy. And Cassidy had never been the jealous type. She didn't like what was happening to her at the hands of Jesse Kirby. She was becoming a person she didn't recognize. As much as her heart screamed in protest, she wondered if she might need to nip this now before she got in any deeper.

Chapter Fifteen

A knock sounded at the door at exactly 6:02, and Cassidy let Jesse in.

"Hey," he said, gauging her.

She gave him a tempered smile, still unsure what was going to happen. Her brain was telling her this needed to end now before she got too out of control of her emotions, but her heart begged her to hear him out with an open mind. She did need to respect him enough to let him say what he had come there to say.

They sat on the couch where Cassidy had a bottle of chardonnay chilling in a carafe. "You want a glass?" she asked.

"No, I'm good," he said, and she started to wonder if he was there to end things with her. Get in and get out. She faced him, her elbow on the back of the couch, letting him speak first.

"I should have told you I had a female roommate. I guess since I see her more as a sister now than anything, I wasn't thinking about it being an issue for you. I just wasn't thinking about it at all."

"You said you see her as a sister now. So, when's the last time you slept with her?"

He thought about it, shaking his head. "I can't really even remember. Maybe last summer?" He nodded. "It was August. And even then it was just a friendly fuck. Her summer session was ending and she was stressed from exams and needed to clear her head and didn't want to swipe right on a stranger. Neither of us was weird at all the next day or any days since. But I didn't feel great about it afterward, and I swore to myself that would be the last time."

"Has she wanted to since then?"

He closed his eyes for a second. "Not until just a few weeks ago. She asked me if I wanted to, and I said no."

"You really didn't want to?" she asked, wanting to believe him, but Cassidy had seen those breasts.

He gave her a half-hearted smile. "It was a couple of days after I met with you at your shop about the cookies. I was interested in you at that point. I didn't want anyone else."

She let her head fall back. "You really have to stop saying this stuff."

"What stuff?"

"The exact right thing at the exact right time."

He smiled, but stayed contrite.

She narrowed her gaze. "Are you at all concerned about the fact that you're her boss? We've got a movement going on around us, you know?"

He shook his head. "It's not like that. Look, I've known her for a few years now. She used to come in the bar before she turned twenty-one and try to flirt her way into getting me to serve her. We sort of became friends. She made friends with all the staff. When she turned twenty-one, we made a big deal of it...had a big party for her. That was the first night she and I slept together. Afterward, she told me her story. She grew up really poor and in a bad situation. Her dad knows she exists but refuses to acknowledge her even though he lives just over in Panama City. She called the Department of Children and Families on her own mom when she was twelve because her mom's boyfriend wouldn't keep his damn hands off of her. And he was one of many. She begged friends to let her spend the night. It broke my heart listening to her."

Cassidy's own heart broke for this young woman, and she was starting to feel like a real Grade-A loser for rushing to judgment of this situation.

"At the time, she'd just gotten downsized for the winter at the restaurant she was waiting tables at, and she was still living with her mom. That's why she was at the bar all the time—just trying to stay away from the drugs and the assholes. I told her she could move in the next day and I gave her a job. She said she'd wanted to go to school but didn't have the money, and even if she did, she wouldn't know how to get started. So I helped her fill out the applications and fronted some of the costs while she got on her feet. She's been in school for two years now. It's actually a great roommate situation. She's really into health and physical fitness so she keeps the groceries stocked and makes all these healthy meals for us. She studies all the time and I read a lot, so we don't really get in each other's way. Look, I've been thinking about another roommate for her. I think the girls who work at the bar would probably squeeze her in at their apartment, but she'd have to start paying rent, and they're pretty out of control. I'm just afraid she'd fall into those patterns and get derailed—"

Cassidy held up a hand, her face flushed with humiliation. "Please, Jesse, stop talking. I'm not at all proud of the way I have behaved today. I've judged you and Gracie when I had no right or place to. It sounds like the two of you have a special friendship, and I would never want to stand in the way of that." She took his hand. "Thank you so much for helping this young woman. You truly are a wonderful man, and I'm lucky to know you."

He visibly relaxed, his shoulders and expression dropping. "Cassidy, I can only imagine what you thought when you saw Gracie this morning. I went upstairs after you left and saw what she had on. She does walk around like that a lot but I'm just so used to it I guess I've become immune to it. I've already talked with her and I asked her to start putting on clothes. I know that sounds crazy, but honestly, I think she's just really proud of her body since she's been doing these barre workouts and she likes to look at herself in the mirror."

She grasped his arm. "If that's what gets her through the day, then please, let her walk around buck naked. I'm serious, Jesse. I feel like such an idiot. I got this all wrong. I hope you'll accept my apology, and I'd like to apologize to her as well. She was kind to me, in her own way, I'm sure, and I acted like a buffoon."

He smiled, looking down at his lap. He took her hand. "I'm sure you did not. Have you eaten dinner yet?"

"No, I haven't."

"Can I take you to dinner?"

"Sure. Actually, this would be our first date, wouldn't it?"

He thought about it. "I guess it is. You've been thrown together with me all the other times, like it or not."

"I'm pretty sure I liked it."

They both stood, and he took her into his arms. "I've missed you these past couple of days."

"I've missed you, too."

They kissed, their own magical recipe, and then he pulled away. "We need to stop or I'm not gonna make it to dinner."

She slid on her sandals that she'd kicked off by the couch. "I'm honestly pretty full from my crow sandwich, but I'll try to make room for more."

Chapter Sixteen

Jesse's new favorite thing to do was share meals with Cassidy. What was his was hers, and what was hers was his, in food at least. They'd eaten dinner together five out of seven nights the past week. He took her out three times, and they ate takeout at her house the other two. If they stayed together a while, one of them would need to learn to cook or else they were both going to end up twenty pounds heavier. He'd be okay with that if it meant he got to stay with her.

She set her fork down on the table. "I can't believe I ate all that. You are fattening me up for the kill, aren't you?"

"Just keeping you happy, baby. Whatever it takes."

She gave him that cute, shy smile she did when she liked something he said to her. He was always afraid he was being cheesy, but if it made her smile at him like that, he didn't care.

His phone rang, an actual call. He checked it and rolled his eyes when he saw it was his sister. He could decline, but then he'd be thinking about it all night. What did she want? Was everyone okay? Not that he cared about his brother and his wife, but he didn't want them to be sick or dead.

Cassidy put her napkin on the table. "I'll let you take that," she said, and then headed toward the restroom.

He answered the call. "Hey, I'm at dinner with someone, but I've got thirty seconds while she's in the restroom. What's going on?"

"So nice to hear from you, Rachel. How's your life these days?" Rachel said.

He rolled his eyes. "I'll call you back later."

"No need. I just wanted to let you know that we're coming to Rosemary Beach for spring break."

He stilled. "When?"

"We leave Saturday."

He switched phone hands, taking in the information. "Why are you just now telling me?"

She let out a sigh. "Because it's all of us."

He clenched his eyes closed. "I assume you mean them."

"I do. I was afraid if I told you in advance then you'd make plans to be gone."

"Is there some reason you're coming here? Something wrong with Hilton Head?"

"We chose Rosemary. I chose it, in fact, because it's the furthest community from Grayton that I could get and stay on 30A."

"Why do you need to be on 30A at all?"

"Hmm, because my brother lives there and I like

to see him more than once a year."

He rubbed his forehead as Cassidy headed his way from across the restaurant. "I'll meet you and your family for dinner but not with *them*."

"I was hoping you would consider coming over for dinner."

"Are you getting just one house?" he asked.

"Mmm hmm," she said weakly.

"Then it's not happening." Cassidy sat down, gauging him curiously. "Look, I'll talk to you about this later."

"Who are you at dinner with? Don't tell me it's an actual date."

"I'll speak with you later."

"Anyone serious?"

"Bye, Rachel." He ended the call and put his phone face down on the table, his heartbeat pounding. He met Cassidy's curious gaze. "My sister."

"Oh," she said, perking up. "I didn't realize you two talked frequently."

"We don't. She was just calling to tell me they're all coming for spring break. They'll be here Saturday, or Sunday, or something." He realized he didn't find out if they were driving or flying.

"Is that…okay?"

"I just don't understand what she's doing."

"Possibly trying to help you and your brother reconcile?"

"By forcing it on me? That's effective." He wadded up his cloth napkin and tossed it onto his plate. "I just wish she wouldn't do this."

"At least she didn't trick you, say it was just her

family and then you get there and it's a sabotage."

"Oh, she knows better than that shit. She did that to me the first Christmas I came to her house. I saw his car in the driveway and just kept on driving right back to Grayton."

"Wow, that was a lot of time spent on the road for nothing." She took his hand. "It takes so much energy to hate a person. I hate to see you grappling with that."

"I want to forgive him and move forward. I really do. But I just can't figure out how I can watch the two of them together, this family unit, kissing one another and smiling like lovebirds. When I imagine that, it feels like a *fuck you* in my face. I think about all the times they were having sex, all the conversations they had with one another about me, feeling guilty, feeling sorry for poor Jesse who was getting fucked by his brother and his girlfriend. I just can't stand it. Can you understand that?"

"I can try. I have tried to put myself in your place, and it wasn't fun, I assure you of that. But have you considered that staying away from them tells them that you aren't over this yet? If you showed up at this house, this mutual territory, more your territory than theirs because they've come to your town…if you show up, you show them that you've risen above what they did to you."

Jesse had thought of this before, but not on those terms. This was his town. They were on his turf. Something about that empowered him. He met her gaze. "Will you come with me?"

Her eyes went wide. He'd taken her off guard. "Oh, well, are you sure? I mean, this is family business. I wouldn't want to intrude."

"I want you there, Cassidy. I'm trying to come along here, but I could really use your support."

She gave him a resigned smile. "Of course I'll come."

He kissed her on the lips and then pulled away. "Thank you."

She nodded and glanced downward, letting her hair cover her face.

Chapter Seventeen

Cassidy had spent longer selecting an outfit for this dinner with Jesse's family than she would have for an audience with the Pope. She wasn't ready for this in any way, shape, or form, but how could she tell him no? The idea that he was even considering being in the room with all of them at once was huge, and she'd talked him into it. How could she abandon him now?

She kept reminding herself that this wasn't about her meeting his family. This was about her supporting him through what was going to be one of the hardest things he'd had to do in a while. She had no idea how she was going to be received by any of them. She didn't even know who all was going to be there. She'd been careful not to ask too many questions, afraid of scaring him off or giving him a reason to change his mind. She was going to be walking into this night completely blind, so her outfit was pretty much the only thing she could control in this situation.

She wanted to go for conservative, but that just made her look older. She tried for trendy, then she was afraid she would look like she was trying too hard to look young. Giving up hope, she called in reinforcements.

The bell rang, and Cassidy opened the door. Maya stood there with a pile of clothing draped across her arm. "Let's do this."

Cassidy had liked Maya since the moment she first met her. She was perfect for Bo, a classic opposites-attract romance. Bo was loud and rowdy. Maya was conservative and buttoned-up, to use Jesse's term. Cassidy wanted Maya for this task for a few reasons. First and most importantly, Maya and Cassidy were about the same size. Maya was probably a tad shorter, but they had the same body type. Secondly, Maya had worked for many years in the corporate world and, quite frankly, made plenty of money and her outer appearance reflected that. While Cassidy dressed a little more on the bohemian side, Maya always looked classy, even when she was dressed down. When Cassidy explained the situation to her, Maya seemed to understand the nuances with great clarity and dropped everything she was doing to get over to Cassidy's house in a pinch. Cassidy would owe her big for this.

Cassidy made way to let Maya in. "How long do we have before he gets here to pick you up?" Maya asked.

"Two hours. Yes, I've spent the day stressing about this."

Maya held up a hand. "Understandably." She pointed between the two bedrooms. "Shall we…"

"Yes, of course." Cassidy motioned Maya to her bedroom. "Can I get you anything to drink?"

"No thank you. I've got a bottle of water in my purse."

Of course she did. Cassidy imagined that Maya was prepared for any and all possibilities and needs at all times. She would make a fantastic mom one day, if that was in her and Bo's plans.

Cassidy led her into the closet. Maya shoved hangers out of the way to make room, hanging all the clothes neatly in a row. "I've got an iron and a steamer in the car in case we need them."

Cassidy nodded, trying to hold in her smile. Boy had she called in the right woman for this job.

"I've got a few options in mind. Since this is a casual dinner at a beach house, I didn't think a dress would be appropriate." She held up a pair of linen pants to Cassidy's legs. "You're a hair taller, so these might not be the appropriate length, but I think they would work for the balance of distinguished lady meets youthful girlfriend." She hung them back on the rack and grabbed another pair of tan, wide-legged pants. "These may be absolutely perfect because I haven't had a chance to get to the tailor yet, but they have been laundered. I can't stand the smell of clothes straight from the store with their pesticides and warehouse stench."

Cassidy took the pants from Maya, realizing how ridiculous she had been to stress the way she had. "These look absolutely perfect. Thank you so much."

"I've got this black top to pair it with, but I was

thinking about that flowy white top you have with the waistband that cuts off about right here," she placed the side of her hand on her stomach, and then pointed at the rack. "May I?"

"Absolutely," Cassidy said, watching Maya flip through her closet. She pulled it out. "Oh yes." She held it up to Cassidy along with the pants. "I think this is it. Would you like to try it on? You can change in there and close me in here and I'll see about some shoes. Are you a ten by any chance?"

"Nine," Cassidy said. "My feet are a little out of proportion with the rest of me."

"Consider yourself lucky. I'm already a ten and I've heard your feet grow during—" She cut herself off, her face going red.

Cassidy just stared at her. "Maya, are you…"

Maya pinched the bridge of her nose, eyes closed tightly. "Oh, God." She wasn't smiling, so Cassidy treaded very lightly. She tugged her by the elbow outside of the closet and they sat on the bed. "I'm sorry," Maya said. "We're trying to focus on you here."

"Screw me," Cassidy said. "What's going on, sweetie?"

"I was pregnant. I found out back in November. Bo and I were through the roof. Our honeymoon baby, we called it. I'd been so worried because I didn't even know if it was possible for me to get pregnant at my age. I mean, I've never even had a scare. But Bo and I had discussed it and we knew it could take a while and with my advanced age, we decided I'd go ahead and get off birth control as soon as we got married, and it worked. Our little miracle."

Cassidy took her hand and squeezed it. "When did you find out you lost the baby?"

"Right before Christmas. We knew not to get excited, and we didn't tell a soul. But we dreamed together, every night, Bo's hand on my belly, rubbing it so sweetly. The look on his face when they told us there wasn't a heartbeat, Cassidy…it about did me in."

Cassidy put her arms around Maya and held her there for a long while, Maya sniffling. "I haven't talked to anyone about this besides Bo. Not even Shayla. We didn't want them to know. This is their time right now. I'm not going to have it watered down by our misfortune."

"What about your sister?" Cassidy asked, knowing that even though she wasn't close to her own sister, a miscarriage was something she may choose to open up to her about.

Maya rolled her eyes. "She's coming down for a visit, which is all I need right now."

"You two aren't close?" Cassidy asked, remembering that Meade was Maya's maid of honor at her wedding.

"We are, I guess, but she's a full mess, Cassidy. She's brilliant. Have I ever told you that? Not like, oh, she's a smart girl, but like, could be a brain surgeon kind of brilliant."

Either Maya had told her that before or someone else had. "That's wonderful."

"It would be if she acted like it. She could be out there curing cancer if she wanted, but instead, she'll tend bar or wait tables. Last year she was working as a blackjack dealer in Vegas. She's thirty-eight years old and she's never had any interest in owning a home or saving for retirement or anything. She lives life like there's no consequences." Maya shook her head, staring off at the wall behind Cassidy. "I finally got her settled in Chicago last year. She's got this really good government job—top secret stuff, security clearances, you name it. But she's starting to complain about it."

"Is it too much pressure?" Cassidy asked.

"Ha!" She doesn't understand the concept of pressure. She leaned in, grabbing Cassidy's arm. "It's too easy for her. She's bored."

"Wow," Cassidy said.

"Oh yeah. I don't know why I'm surprised. This is what she does. She tries to live up to her potential, and then she blows it up within months." She shook her head. "I know she's going to quit. It's just a matter of time." She squeezed her eyes shut. "I can't worry about this right now. I'm trying so hard to take care of myself. The doctor said we could try again right away, and so we're doing that, God, how we're doing that. I'm that whole ovulation monitoring cliché. I'm reading endless materials about it. I'm taking my temperature, I've got like three apps on my phone that are supposedly helping me. And I'm trying to freaking figure out what I did to mess the first one up so I won't do that again."

"Sweetheart, I know less about pregnancy than anyone on the planet, but one thing I'd bet my life on is that you didn't do anything to mess that pregnancy up. I don't know anyone who eats cleaner or takes better care of their body than you do."

She closed her eyes. "I know that. It's just hard to

understand why, you know?"

Cassidy nodded. "I do know."

Maya let out a sigh. "Well, now that that's all out. Let's get you dressed."

Cassidy took her hand again. "You are doing wonderful, my friend. Whatever happens, you've got a support system around you to help you through it. And I'd say Shayla would be more upset knowing you were holding this in than she would be if you told her what you were going through."

Maya nodded, swiping at a tear. "I know. I'm going to tell her soon."

"The wedding was yesterday, wasn't it?" Cassidy asked, just now remembering. God, she had to get out of her own self-absorbed head.

Maya smiled. "It was so lovely. Simple but beautiful. It couldn't have suited them more perfectly."

Cassidy nodded, feeling a tear form in her own eye. Damn emotions. "I have no doubt."

Maya let out a laugh. "Chase bawled through the whole thing."

With that, a tear fell right down Cassidy's cheek and she laughed along with Maya. "Of course he did."

"We're some lucky folks in this group, having found one another." Maya squeezed Cassidy's hand. "All of us."

Cassidy nodded, the tears free-falling now. They both broke out in huge smiles and hugged each other again. Cassidy pulled away. "Okay, enough of all that. My eyes are gonna look like puffed-up marshmallows."

Maya held up a finger as she dabbed her eyes with a tissue. "I have something for that in my bag."

Cassidy smiled and they went back to work on the outfit.

Chapter Eighteen

Jesse and Cassidy held hands wordlessly the whole way down 30A to the house in Rosemary. As GPS weaved them through the rows of white houses with brown trim, Jesse's stomach tied itself into tight knots he wasn't sure he'd ever be able to loosen.

Cassidy pointed. "I think that's it."

He parked behind a car with Kentucky plates that he didn't recognize but assumed was one of theirs. As he cut off the engine, he looked over at her. "Thank you for coming."

"Of course," she said, giving him a comforting smile.

As they got out of the car and walked toward the door, his whole body filled with an almost paralyzing anxiety. Part of the reason he'd wanted Cassidy there with him was because he knew he wouldn't back out with her there. Otherwise, he was pretty sure he'd be outta there.

The front door stood open, a glass screen door in place. Just as Jesse was getting ready to knock on it, his sister passed by chasing one of the kids. She caught sight of Jesse and Cassidy, surprise changing her firm expression. He just stood there, waiting for her.

"We got this," Cassidy said out of the corner of her mouth, and just her use of the plural pronoun was enough to get him through the next five minutes.

The door opened and his sister stood there with that know-it-all half-smile she wore around him— the one that always made him feel like a kid.

Ava and Olivia pushed through the doorway and attacked him. "Did you bring us anything?"

"Girls," Rachel barked, and then nudged them out of the way, putting her arms around Jesse. "Thank you for coming," she said into his ear.

He stepped back from her. "Rachel, this is Cassidy. We're..." He trailed off, realizing they had never established what they were, and he hadn't thought about how he'd introduce her. "We're together," he said.

Rachel blinked, staring at Cassidy for way too long. Jesse put a protective arm around Cassidy, reinforcing his stance with her.

"It's so nice to meet you." Cassidy offered the pink boxes she held. "I brought a couple of pies. I run a bakery in Seaside."

"Oh," Rachel said. "How lovely. Thank you. Please, come in."

As they stepped into the entryway, Rachel fussed at the girls and then yelled for Elijah to get off the game.

Cassidy leaned in. "Did she know I was coming?"

"Yeah, I told her I was bringing someone with me."

"Did you tell her I was older?"

"No, fuck that." If Rachel or any of them had a problem with Cassidy, he'd be more than happy for the two of them to leave immediately.

Rachel turned back to them. "Come in, please. Everyone's in the kitchen...except Chuck. His golf game's running long, but he'll be here eventually."

Jesse's feet could barely move him forward. Cassidy took his hand and he gripped the wine bottle in his other hand.

They rounded the corner to find his brother, a good thirty or forty pounds heavier than Jesse had last seen him, standing next to a highchair holding a bottle of beer while a woman with short brown hair whose body he didn't recognize situated a baby into it. "He is not too big for a highchair. It amazes me that you think you—"

"Lauren," his brother said, cutting her off.

"What?" she asked, looking up at him with a disdain Jesse wasn't sure he'd ever seen in her eyes. Justin nodded at Jesse, and she turned to see him.

"Oh. I didn't hear the door," Lauren said, her face losing color as she set her gaze on Jesse.

"I found them on the doorstep," Rachel said. "Cassidy, this is Lauren and Justin, Jesse's brother."

Jesse gave his sister a look. Either she was acting like she assumed Cassidy wasn't important enough to know who was who, or she was trying to drive the point home that Jesse and Justin were brothers and needed to get over it.

"It's so nice to meet you all," Cassidy said with her calming, gracious way.

Justin gauged Jesse from across the room, feeling him out. Jesse wasn't about to let him off the hook, not for a second. Justin nodded. "Hey."

"Mmm," Jesse uttered.

Lauren checked on the baby and then walked across the room and shook Cassidy's hand. "It's very nice to meet you."

"Cassidy has a bakery in…Seaside, was it?" Rachel asked.

Lauren looked at her curiously. "Not Seaside Sweets?"

Cassidy smiled. "Yes, that's the one."

"We were in there yesterday." Lauren turned to Rachel. "That's the one I was telling you about where we got the cinnamon rolls."

"Okay," Rachel said, nodding but seeming less impressed than Lauren was, of course.

"A very pretty blond girl helped us."

"That's Marigold," Cassidy said. "She's my assistant manager and lifesaver. I don't know how I ever did it without her."

"She helped us organize this whole week. She wrote down a list of places we had to try and all kinds of stuff for the kids to do."

Cassidy grinned with a nod. "That's Marigold. She's a people person."

Jesse wasn't sure what was happening here, but he wasn't digging it. He didn't need Cassidy and Lauren to be friendly.

Lauren finally met Jesse's gaze. "Hey, Jesse," she said, and then to his horror, she opened her arms and tried to pull him in for a hug. They ended up in an awkward half-hug with him holding her off by the arm. He understood her need to lighten an awkward situation, but he wasn't ready for touching.

Lauren pulled away and swiped at her forehead looking embarrassed. "Well, I hope you both came hungry. We're boiling a big pot of shrimp, and we've got potatoes and green beans—"

"Did Mom come?" Jesse asked, not able to take the fakeness of talking about what was for dinner.

"She didn't," Rachel said. "Pete can't really travel in the car anymore with his back, and you know Mom's thoughts on flying."

Jesse nodded, still not used to his new stepdad, though they'd probably been together seven or eight years now.

They all stood there in silent hell, trying to figure out what to say next. Cassidy saved them. "What can I do to help with dinner?"

"Nothing," Rachel said, taking the bottle of wine Jesse was still holding.

"That's from Cassidy," Jesse said.

Rachel turned to Cassidy. "Thank you. That's really too much with the pies."

"All right, fuck this. I can't stand this," Justin said.

"Justin!" Lauren shouted, indicating the kid.

"He's a fucking baby."

Rachel got up in his face. "Do you mind?"

"The kids are all outside."

"But I'm here, and so are others who might not want to hear your foul—"

Justin muscled away from her. "Jesse? Please, can we talk?" his brother asked, a look in his eye of desperation.

Jesse, a little dumbfounded by the animosity in the room, just nodded. All this time he'd imagined Justin and Rachel laughing and living it up in romantic bliss in his absence. Maybe he had it wrong. He turned to Cassidy. "Is that okay?"

"Of course. I'm looking forward to getting to know Rachel and Lauren."

When they got out the front door, Justin turned to him. "Wanna take a walk?"

"Please," Jesse said, eyeing the house which seemed to pulse with anger.

They walked by a few houses before either of them spoke. Justin was the first. "I know I've said this before, but I can't say it enough. I'm fucking sorry, man."

Jesse wondered if he meant he was sorry for what he'd done to Jesse, or sorry for marrying Lauren. Either way, he didn't respond.

Justin shook his head, glancing around. "Love is so fucked up. You get in that headspace and it's like you lose your goddamned mind. I was just so miserable all the time, for years. I tried dating other girls, but I couldn't get her off my mind. I look back now, and I can't believe I did that to my own brother, but when I think back, hard, I remember that I was desperate, and those feelings for her just wouldn't quit. I imagined you marrying her and I wanted to blow my brains out."

"Fuck," Jesse said, a little disturbed.

"I wish I was goddamned joking. But now..." He shook his head.

Jesse knew he should feel vindicated, but that

victory wasn't nearly as sweet as it should have been.

"I just want out," Justin said.

Jesse stopped. "Are you fucking kidding me?"

Justin turned to face him, looking surprised.

"You took her from me. You married her. I had to leave my cushy job because of you. And now you're ready to throw her out?"

"I'm not gonna throw her out. I'd be the one leaving."

"What about your kid? And is she pregnant now?"

His brother gave a sardonic laugh. "Nope, that's just her new body."

Jesse eyed him hard. "You know you didn't age too well either, asshole. What have you put on, thirty pounds?"

"I can't believe you're defending her."

"From her husband making a snide comment about her weight. Fuck yeah I am."

"It's not just the weight gain. It's the constant nagging and bitching. Do this, do that, don't do it that way."

"Well when I walked in the house tonight it looked like you were telling her she was doing something wrong with that highchair."

"Yeah, because I have to. I feel my manhood slipping away sometimes." He backhanded Jesse in the arm. "Look at you. You look like a goddamned million bucks. You own your own bar at the beach. Who the fuck do you think won here?"

"I'm sorry, were we playing a game?"

Justin waved him off. "Just fucking forget it all." He glanced around like he didn't know what direction to walk in.

"You've got a wife who loves you and a baby at home. You're not fucking that up. You've been selfish your whole damned life. Justin, Justin, Justin. That's all you've ever cared about or thought about. And nothing has ever been good enough for you. You always want what someone else has, and when you can't make it for yourself, you take it. Well, fuck you. My life's not for the taking anymore, big brother. And yours isn't for the leaving. You say you think you're losing your manhood? This talk of leaving her with that baby makes you a whiny little immature brat of a boy. Man the fuck up."

Justin hauled back for a punch but Jesse had spent too many afternoons in the gym not to see it coming and ducked. Justin lost his balance and fell to the ground, and Jesse realized he was probably already drunk. He'd likely been drinking all day on the beach while Rachel and Lauren took care of the kids.

"Fuck you!" Justin shouted from the front yard of some family's home. A salty looking old man walked out the front door eyeing Jesse, who just held a hand up in apology and headed back toward the house.

"You get back here and face me you chicken shit," Justin shouted.

"You get the hell off this lawn, you drunk idiot," shouted the old man.

Jesse was almost back to the house when heavy and quick footsteps behind him got his attention, and he ducked away from Justin's charge. Justin toppled over again, this time bouncing off a car parked in the road, denting it with a thud to rock Rosemary, and then landing on the sidewalk. As appealing as the idea of beating the hell out of him was, he knew if he laid a hand on him, Rachel would turn this all around on him. Jesse would somehow be the asshole again, and he was tired of being the asshole.

Jesse flung open the door and marched into the kitchen to find the women all three looking stunned. "What was that noise?" Rachel asked.

"Justin. He fell into a car." He turned to Lauren. "Hope you've got your insurance card."

"Did you shove him into it?" Rachel asked, as she headed toward the front door. Typical Rachel. Everything was Jesse's fault even when it wasn't.

"Wish I could take credit for it, but he did it all to himself," he said, mainly for Cassidy's benefit. Rachel wasn't even in earshot anymore. "You ready?" he asked Cassidy.

She nodded, eyes still wide.

Lauren's face contorted, and the fact that she wasn't even going to check on her husband spoke volumes. The kid sat in the highchair throwing handfuls of cereal at her, and she just took it like a punishment.

Jesse gathered her into his arms. "I'm sorry," he said softly, into her ear. When he pulled away, she gave him a look, begging him to save her. But there was nothing Jesse could do for her, not anymore.

Jesse grabbed the bottle of wine and then Cassidy's hand and headed to the front door. When they got outside, Rachel and Justin were in a scuffup with the guy whose SUV had been assaulted.

"I saw the whole thing," said the salty old man, arms crossed, up in the mix.

"Do you think we need to—?"

Jesse cut Cassidy off. "No."

They jumped in his car and backed out of the drive. When they got safely on 30A, Jesse turned to Cassidy, his heart pounding. "I love you."

He put his eyes back on the road, and they drove wordlessly to her house.

Jesse had entered somewhat of a catatonic state. He sat on Cassidy's couch with a beer in his hand watching HGTV. It'd been on that channel whenever Cassidy turned on the TV. Even though she'd handed Jesse the remote, he didn't use it. She wasn't sure he even understood that he was holding it. Luckily, she had been to the store that previous day and had the stuff to make tortilla soup, so that's what she had chosen to do with her hands. Lord knew she needed to occupy them.

Whatever had gone down between Jesse and his brother had disturbed him deeply. The fact that he'd wrapped his arms around Lauren like a father would a troubled teen worried Cassidy. These weren't her people and they weren't her problems, but whatever was happening between Lauren and her husband was hard not to be concerned about.

Jesse had turned off his phone. It'd rang once when they'd gotten to her house and he'd silenced it and then put his attention back on the television. Cassidy stirred the soup, peering in to see him, and then turned off the burner and covered the pan.

The fact that he'd told her he loved her didn't mean much to her. She understood the meaning behind it. *These people make me miserable. I don't want to be like them. I want to be like us.* He hadn't said those words, but she'd bet money that's what he'd meant.

She sat down beside him and put her hand on his thigh. He dropped the remote and covered her hand with his, trying to force a smile. "The soup is ready if you're hungry," she said.

"I'm not. Please, go ahead and eat though."

"I'm not either. We'll eat it later in the week."

He met her gaze. "You think you'll want me around later in the week?"

She wrapped her hand around his thigh. "If I left you after witnessing one fight with you and your family, I'd be pretty sorry."

He squinted at the wall. "What a goddamned shit-show. Lauren's dad would be humiliated if he witnessed that."

"Who knows what he's witnessed in the past several years," she said.

Jesse huffed a humorless laugh. "God, you're right. There's no telling what he thinks about Justin."

"He seemed pretty drunk," Cassidy said.

"I didn't even notice until he took a swing at me and fell on his ass."

Cassidy's stomach flipped. "He hit you?"

"He tried, twice actually. Well, the second time he just tried to charge me like a bull."

"Have you two always been like that with one another?"

"When we were kids. Not since we've been adults. But I guess he's been getting one over on me since we were about nineteen and twenty-one, so I'm guessing he didn't have to get physical with me before tonight." He re-gripped his beer. "He had the nerve to call her fat."

Cassidy's heart hurt for that poor girl. "He didn't," she said, unbelieving.

"I thought she was pregnant. He said he wanted to leave her, and I asked how he could leave his own kid and if she was pregnant. You should have seen the look on that asshole's face. Like he was disgusted with his own wife." He shook his head. "I just can't believe I've wasted all these years of energy on hating that worthless piece of shit."

She squeezed his hand, feeling like though this was tough now, he was turning a corner of some sort.

He stared off at the wall. "This is fucked up, but I keep wondering if we would have been some version of all that if I'd stayed with her."

"No way. You're entirely too good of a man."

"Maybe we wouldn't have had the anger, but would we have had the resentment? Is that what kids do to a marriage, or is that what parents do to each other?"

Cassidy smiled. "If we had the answer to that, we could make a lot of money selling the secret."

"Can we just go to bed?" he asked.

She nodded, and they both stood. She didn't know if he meant to make love or just to sleep. Either way, she was fine with it. After they both undressed in no rush, he pulled the sheets back while she hung up Maya's pants and her blouse. They slid into the bed, and he nudged her onto her side and spooned in behind her. She closed her eyes as she laid her arm over the top of his, drinking in his naked body against hers. But this time, there was nothing sexual about it. All she felt surrounding the two of them was pure, sweet affection.

Chapter Nineteen

Jesse hid out at Cassidy's house the rest of the week, and Cassidy couldn't blame him. His family knew where his bar was, but they didn't know where her house was. Even though a part of her wished there was a way to work things out with them, she understood that wasn't going to happen right then.

She and Jesse had gotten into a rhythm together. He'd get up at the crack of dawn with her and they'd have breakfast, then she'd go to the shop while he went into the bar and took care of anything that needed to be done in the early morning hours. Then they'd hookup back at her place and spend the rest of the afternoon together. He said he was calling it his vacation and that he hadn't taken one in years.

Selfishly, she'd been luxuriating in him all week long. Marigold had been filled in on the story and was more than happy to go solo each day from about two o'clock on while Cassidy went home and spent the afternoons in bed with Jesse. Cassidy had never been naked so much in her life. Jesse was ready to go all the time, sometimes barely letting her get through the door before sweeping her off to the bedroom. Cassidy was aware there was something cathartic going on here. Her body was acting as a sort of medicine for his weakened soul. She was more than happy to provide it.

"You're sure you've got this?" Cassidy asked Marigold.

"Yes, go get naked with the hot guy."

Cassidy grinned at her, and then that grin faded when the front door to the shop opened and in walked Lauren and Rachel. She plastered it back on. "Hello, ladies."

Marigold pointed. "Hey, how did your week go?"

Lauren tried hard with a smile. "It was lovely. Thank you so much for all your recommendations. We did a ton of that stuff. Especially all the kid stuff."

"That's wonderful," Marigold said and then turned to Cassidy. "This kind lady was in the shop earlier this week."

"Yes, I heard," Cassidy said. "This is actually Jesse's sister-in-law Lauren, and this is his sister Rachel."

Marigold, who grew up with things like charm school and cotillion, didn't miss a beat. "Oh, how nice. I'm so glad to make the connection."

Lauren turned to Cassidy. "We've come to apologize about how things went down the other night. You must know that is not typical of our family."

Cassidy held up both hands. "Families are complicated. I get it."

Rachel stayed tight-lipped and straight-faced, making Cassidy a bit uncomfortable. "We were hoping to say goodbye to Jesse. We're leaving tomorrow. But he's not been at the bar the few times we've stopped by, and he's not responding to his phone. Is there any way you'd consider relaying a message to him, or letting him know we'd like to talk?"

"I can certainly do that," Cassidy said, meaning it, but knowing there wasn't a chance in hell he'd call either of them.

Lauren smiled. "That would be very kind of you. We'd really appreciate it." A look passed between Rachel and Lauren, and then Lauren turned to Marigold, seeming a little uncomfortable. "Um, would it be possible for you to take a break with me for a second? I just wanted to get a little information about the area."

This was very possibly a setup orchestrated by Rachel. Cassidy had only spent a handful of minutes with her the other day, but she'd been on the playground enough in her day to see how bullies operated.

Marigold passed her own look to Cassidy, who gave her a reassuring nod in return. "Sure," Marigold said. "Let's walk out to the bench outside. It's a beautiful day."

Left alone, Cassidy prepped for battle, because she felt one coming on. "Would you like a coffee or an iced tea?"

"No thanks. But I would like to talk to you about

Jesse."

"Okay," Cassidy said. The polite thing to do would be to offer her a seat at a table, but Cassidy was just fine behind the counter. She leaned on it, a move showing she wasn't backing away.

"I have a feeling you had something to do with Jesse being willing to come the other night. Am I correct?"

Cassidy shrugged, not willing to give up any information Jesse may or may not want divulged.

"Well, thank you. That's certainly further than I've been able to get with him, but I imagine you have a little different hold over him than I do." There it was—some sort of back-handed compliment turned insult.

Cassidy remained quiet, holding Rachel's stare.

"I'm really sorry you didn't get to meet our mother. She would have liked that, I'm sure."

"I'm sorry about that, too," Cassidy said.

Rachel's expression turned, and Cassidy could feel the slingshot raring back. "I probably do need to apologize for the shock on my face when I met you. You are definitely not who I pictured Jesse would bring."

Cassidy kept her expression pleasant, just waiting her out. Cassidy could see her silence was incensing this woman.

Rachel came closer. "I'm not sure if he's told you, but Jesse is twenty-nine."

"I am aware," Cassidy said.

"He's always wanted to be a father. Did he tell you about the miscarriage?"

Cassidy had played enough poker in her life to

know not to blink. She smiled. "It was good seeing you again, Rachel. I'll walk you out."

She came around the corner and headed for the door, hoping she was coming off less flustered than she felt. Rachel stood in front of the door. "It's important that we see Jesse before we leave. We are his family."

"Understood."

Rachel gave her a mustache-twirling smile. "I'm not sure what your end game is here, but this family wants Jesse to be happy, and that will include a wife that's his own age and as many children as his heart desires."

Cassidy reached around her and pushed the door open. "Nice to see you, Rachel." She held up a hand to Lauren on the bench with Marigold. "Good to see you again, Lauren."

Lauren gave a reluctant smile, and she and Rachel headed to their car. Once they were safely on the road, Cassidy headed back inside and closed her eyes, letting herself breathe deeply to calm her nerves.

Marigold rubbed Cassidy's back. "Something tells me that wasn't a friendly visit."

Cassidy reached over and patted Marigold's shoulder. "They just love and care for him. It's fine." She walked away, heading toward the back, not stopping until she got to the bathroom where she could close herself off for a minute and let the news she'd just been delivered sink in.

When Cassidy opened the door to her house, Jesse shouted, "I'm naked. You've been warned."

She smiled and dropped her purse on the couch on the way to the bedroom. He was not kidding. He lay on his side, his long body stretched down her bed, a hardback book in his hand. She was pretty certain this was the sexiest sight she had or ever would see in her lifetime. He put the bookmark in place and laid the book on the nightstand.

"How's the story?" she asked.

"Better the second go-around."

She glanced at the title. "*The Great Train Robbery*," she read as she lifted off her shirt and bra in one motion.

"Yep. They're starting to know me by name at the library."

She wiggled out of her shorts and underwear. "I'll go with you next time and you can help me pick something out. Then you'll have to keep me awake at night so I can read it." She hiked her leg over his body so she was straddling him.

"I can definitely keep you awake at night," he said, grasping her thighs and rubbing up them.

"Mmm," she uttered, her eyes closed. She loved it when he rubbed on her. She pulled her hair out of the ponytail holder, letting it fall free.

"You have no idea how sexy it is when you do that."

"I'm fairly sure it doesn't match how sexy you look naked in my bed with a book." She reached down and kissed him, and then rolled over onto her back.

He climbed on top of her. "You don't like it on top, do you?"

She smiled. "You figured that out?"

"Well, after a few dozen times, yeah."

"I can't help it," she said rubbing up and down his back. "I like to feel your weight on me. It makes me feel…dominated."

"Oh, yeah," he said, kissing her. "'Cause I'm such a big strong man?" he asked with a grin.

"Mmm hmm," she said, grinning back. "I've been single a long time. I've got to be the man and the woman in my life on a daily basis. I like to be on bottom in bed. Or maybe I'm just too tired and want you to do all the work."

"Baby, I'll work on you anytime you want."

He moved down her body giving one of her breasts a quick kiss on the way, but they'd passed the point of languidly teasing each other with trails of kisses in erogenous zones. They wanted to be satisfied and they wanted it now. They'd become selfish that way, spoiling one another.

She opened her legs for him and relaxed back, moaning with his efforts, which was something she did only with him. He seemed to like it when she vocally expressed her pleasure, and it definitely showed him what he was doing very right.

He stopped before she got too out of hand and slid up her body, pressing his hard cock against her center. "I want you to come with me."

She nodded, obediently. "I can handle that task." She waited while he rolled the condom on which he could do faster than any man she'd ever been with. He guided himself inside of her, slow and steady, relaxed from his afternoon of reading naked, she presumed. He kissed her as he moved inside of her, and she wasn't sure what she liked more, his cock inside of her or his mouth on hers. Both would do just fine.

He took his time, making every single move count with both his mouth and his body. "Are you close?" he asked.

"I could let you do this to me all day."

He smiled. "I'll wait then."

She had never known a man who could control himself the way he could. Given, when they first started this, way back on the beach which felt like an eternity ago, he was quicker on the draw. But now that they'd had an inordinate amount of practice, he was beyond skilled.

The pressure built inside of her enough that she was ready for the release. She nodded, and he took her cue, moving faster and harder into her. As he watched her, she made sure to let him see in her face what he was doing to her, and she let go with a wail, him following suit right behind her.

He fell into the crook of her neck like he always did. That was almost her favorite part of making love with him—the after-kisses. "There is nowhere on earth I'd rather be than inside you," he whispered, and she closed her eyes, letting the weight of him crush her, wishing she could somehow get even closer to him. She was falling hard and fast, there was no doubt about that.

"Don't move a muscle," he said. "I'll be right back."

As she waited for him to return from the bathroom, the irritation in the back of her mind moved to the forefront. She wasn't going to keep any secrets from him, nothing of significance, and his family's visit to her shop was significant.

He slid into the bed and pulled the sheet over them, moaning as he ran his hand over her hip and around to her ass. "Touching your body never gets old. I think it somehow gets more intense for me every time I touch you."

She ran the back of her fingertips down his chest. "I feel the same way."

He closed his eyes, taking in her touch. He opened them, searching hers like he had something to say. Was this going to be the moment he told her he loved her for real? He hadn't said it since Monday night, but she'd felt it from him all week. She didn't want to hear this from him now, not when she had to talk about his family. "Do you like boats?" he asked.

She let out a relieved breath. "Mmm hmm."

"I'd like to take you out on my boat. For the record, I've taken a few women out on that boat for the purposes of seduction, but this time, I just want to take you out on my ocean."

She grinned. "Your ocean?"

"Oh, hell yeah it's mine. When I'm on it, whether it's on a paddleboard or in a boat or parasailing above it, it's mine. It calms me. It's the most wholly fulfilling thing on the planet."

She narrowed her gaze. "Are you sure you're just twenty-nine? Because you don't seem like any other twenty-nine-year-old I know."

"It's all the books. They screw up my vocabulary."

She kissed him, loving him, truly. "Sometimes I can't believe you're mine," she said, hoping she hadn't overstepped. They'd not actually claimed to be exclusive yet, but she hoped it was understood. Her insecurity felt the need to test him.

"Sometimes?" he asked. "I feel that way every moment of every day."

It was so hard for her to believe that this passionate young man had been sleeping around for years. He didn't seem capable of a quickie with a woman.

"How was work?" he asked, brushing his fingertips over her breast.

She let out a resigned breath. "It was fine until right before I came home. Rachel and Lauren came by."

He rolled his eyes. "That shouldn't surprise me, I guess. What did they want?"

"They wanted me to give you the message that they need to talk to you before they leave."

"I gleaned that from the numerous texts and messages. Were they kind to you?"

"Lauren was sweet. I think she's bonded with Marigold."

"What about Rachel?" he asked, seeming to know the answer.

Cassidy had to tread lightly here. Rachel was his sister. He might know how she could be, but he loved her, and she was like a mother figure to him. On the other hand, Cassidy wasn't going to keep secrets from him. "Rachel was protective of you, understandably."

Concern crossed his expression. "What'd she say to you?"

"Nothing of importance, except one thing she mentioned that I think was meant to test me. She wanted to make sure I knew you wanted kids."

He rolled over and put his wrist on his forehead. "Fuck. I can't believe she did that."

"She asked if I knew about the miscarriage," Cassidy said on a wing and a prayer.

He closed his eyes tightly, shaking his head, and Cassidy couldn't tell if he was upset or furious. He sat up. "Goddammit. It was not her place to tell you that."

She sat up with him. "I'm sorry. I didn't want to keep that from you."

"No, I'm glad you told me." He thought about it, narrowing his gaze. "She wanted you to tell me she told you that. She wanted to get a rise out of me so I'd call her or go down there. Fuck her. I'm done here."

Cassidy wasn't sure how to advise Jesse, so she wouldn't. She was never a fan of phrases like *family is everything* because she'd known plenty of people in her lifetime who had no family. If family was everything, where did that leave those people? And what if your family were assholes? Jesse wanting to be clear from them might be the right solution here. He'd tried to reconcile and it ended in damage to someone's car and him holing up in her house for a week. These weren't people who uplifted his spirit.

She squeezed his thigh, letting him know she cared.

"It upset me, okay?" he said. "Lauren was pregnant and she lost the baby. Rachel was there at the hospital, and I cried with her. I was scared not only for the baby but for Lauren. I can't believe she brought this up with you."

"I'm so sorry, Jesse," Cassidy said, her heart breaking for him. She thought about Bo rubbing Maya's pregnant belly, and she almost lost it. But she had to stay tear-free for Jesse right now.

He shook his head, and Cassidy could see the fury building. "That was my story to tell when the time was right for me to tell it."

Cassidy nodded, making sure he knew she was on his side, but not daring to say another word in this moment.

He huffed a humorless laugh. "After I found out about them, I realized it probably wasn't even mine. I remember thinking we hadn't even been having sex much at the time she got pregnant, but I didn't understand the timelines and how it all worked, something about counting the pregnancy from the first day of the last period. The whole thing confused the hell out of me. And I think Lauren kept the timeline purposefully ambiguous, knowing whose baby it was. That's why I didn't tell you. I doubt it was even mine."

"But you thought it was at the time," Cassidy said.

"I also thought my girlfriend was faithful."

"Had you two been trying for a baby?"

"Fuck no. She was still in law school. She was on the pill, but apparently she'd missed a couple of days. Sometimes I wonder if that wasn't her way out. Get pregnant with his baby and then we'd have to split up."

Cassidy sat with her legs crossed, facing him. "Is that something you wanted back then, a baby?"

"No, I was scared shitless when she said she was pregnant. I mean, I knew it would happen eventually, but I was thinking that wouldn't be coming for years. I was only twenty-two at the time."

"What about now? Would you want a baby now?" she asked.

"Not after seeing what it's done to them."

She swallowed a big lump down her throat. "What about before you saw that. Are children something you want?"

"Not right this minute, no."

She closed her eyes tightly, and he grabbed her knee. "Don't do that. Don't look like that. This is exactly what Rachel wanted. Us to have this stupid conversation."

"It's not stupid, Jesse. It's extremely important. I'm forty-four years old. I know there are women my age who get pregnant all the time, but there are huge risks involved, and I'll be quite honest, I'm not willing to take those risks. If kids are something you want or you even think you might want, we need to end this now before—"

"No." He took her hands. "The reason I wanted to take you out on the boat tomorrow is because I wanted to tell you I'm in love with you."

Cassidy's heart practically leapt out of her chest.

"I wanted to tell you out on the ocean in my favorite place on earth with nobody around us and my family long gone away from this place. I wanted to tell you during a moment that we'd never forget for the rest of our lives, but fuck it. I'll tell you again tomorrow, and the next day, and the next day…every day for fucking ever."

Pressure mounted behind Cassidy's eyes, and the tears came quicker than she could try to stop them.

He smiled, wiping them away with his thumbs and then holding her head in his hands. He moved his hands down to her shoulders and squeezed. "I have met so many women over these past few years, and you are so completely unique and special. I wake up every day in this bed with you, and I have to pinch myself. I can't believe you're real. I can't believe we're real. Look, I'm not going to sit here and tell you that I'm never going to want a child. There's no way I can know how I'm going to feel in five or ten years. But what I know right now is that you have made me into a whole man again. I've spent the last seven years fucking off and fucking around, miserable on the inside." He took her hand and pressed it against his heart. "But you've opened my heart. You've shined a light inside my dark soul, and fuck it if that sounds cheesy. That's how I feel."

Their mouths met, hands threading through each other's hair as they clumsily found their way back to a horizontal position. She found his cock and within seconds it was ready for her. He went for the nightstand, and she took his arm. He met her gaze and she shook her head. "I want to feel you inside of me."

He blinked. "We can? I mean, you're—"

"I'm on birth control."

Jesse kissed her, slowing down, every touch of his mouth against hers a deliberate motion. "I love you," he said.

The words were right there on the tip of her tongue. She felt it. She felt infinitesimal amounts of love for this beautiful man, but she couldn't say the words. Not right then.

He pushed inside of her, and she let out a pleasured moan at the feel of his bare skin inside of her.

"Oh, fuck, Cassidy. I'm not going to last."

"Let yourself go," she said, her heart so full of emotion she could almost feel it bursting.

True to his word, he collapsed on top of her, but this time, he didn't roll off to head to the bathroom. This time, he just moved a little to the side, taking his weight off of her, and they lay there like that, their bodies melded into one.

Chapter Twenty

Seanna, Maya, Shayla, Marigold, and Cassidy sat on the beach watching the five sexiest men alive play volleyball. At least to these ladies, they were the sexiest men alive, but Cassidy figured there were at least a few other women on the beach that day that didn't mind the view.

"God, we're lucky," Seanna said. "Look at those bods."

Bo set Jesse up, and he jumped high in the air for a spike.

"That's like too hot to be legal, or something," Marigold said.

"I see guys that look like this all the time at the gym," Maya said. When they all slid her a look, she said, "I'm kidding. Look at them. It's like that scene in *Top Gun* but hotter."

Jesse and Bo did a high five thing, and then Jesse grinned over at Cassidy, giving a bow.

"Ah, look at your man peacocking for you, Cassidy," Seanna said. "So adorable."

Cassidy smiled over at her niece who she couldn't adore more if she tried. Seanna had been so casual about this thing with Jesse, who was about two years younger than Seanna was. Cassidy had asked her one day when she'd come in the shop if she was okay with it, and Seanna had hugged her and told her as long as she was happy and being treated right, she was okay with any person Cassidy chose.

Ever since the day Jesse had told Cassidy he loved her, the two of them had been floating in some sort of undiscovered dimension. She'd thought she'd had some loves in her life, but she hadn't had a clue. This young guy was showing her a love she'd never dreamed could exist.

But she'd been careful not to say it back. As much as she was allowing herself to indulge in this relationship, she couldn't get past the idea that she was being selfish. Jesse could be with someone else, someone younger who he could live a traditional life with. Someone who could bear his children should he decide that was what he wanted someday.

On the other hand, the idea that she had helped to pull him out of a bad place into one of happiness couldn't be denied. Leaving him now with instructions to go find the *real one* seemed ludicrous and damaging. Not to mention the fact that she was happier than she'd been in ages. It was working for the moment, and she was indulging in that moment, but the undeniable obstacles kept her from telling Jesse just exactly how in love with him she was.

Cassidy's phone dinged, and she read the text.

Hey, we're in Miramar to meet with a potential donor. Would love to see you. Meet for dinner tomorrow night?

Cassidy looked up to see Jesse and Bo work together like professional athletes. She didn't need his permission to meet up with Ingrid and Noel, but it would be courteous to mention it before she solidified. She and Jesse didn't have plans, per se, but they'd been spending every moment outside of work together for the past month.

"Everything okay?" Shayla asked, sitting beside her.

"Oh, sure." Cassidy smiled at her.

The guys finished their game, Bo and Jesse proudly bragging about how they defeated Dane, Chase, and Blake even being down a man on their side. They all settled around the girls, some of them collapsing under the tent they had set up. Jesse held out his hand to Cassidy. "Wanna walk with me?"

She let him pull her up, and they headed down the beach. She was turning into a full-on mid-life-crisis cliché. She and Jesse had gone shopping, and he'd talked her into a bikini, of all things. She hadn't worn one in years. She felt like she was walking down the beach in her bra and underwear.

"When's the last time you took a beach day?" he asked.

"I can't even remember. What about you?"

"With friends, it's been a long time. But I take my paddleboard out by myself enough."

"I've got to see you on one of those things."

"I doubt I look hot. It's a whole lot of balancing."

"I'm sure you look sexy doing it. It'd be hard for

you not to even if you tried."

He smiled at her and then put his gaze back on the beach in front of them. "You can't ever break up with me. I like your friends too much."

"At this point, I think you're a bigger part of the group than I am. They certainly like you more."

"They just like me because I get you out of the house." He pointed in front of them. "Crab."

"I love those. They're so funny how they crawl back in the sand so fast."

"You're probably stepping on one now and don't even know it."

"Oh no," she said, high-stepping for effect.

He grabbed her and pulled her into his arms. "You are the hottest woman on this beach."

"I can't believe you talked me into a bikini. I feel naked."

He ran his hands over her ass. "I wish you were naked."

She peered around him. "Hands up higher, boy. My niece is over there."

"I think she may suspect you're having sex with me."

"Well of course she does, but we don't need to solidify that thought."

"How can I be expected to keep my hands off of you when you're looking like this? That's just evil torture."

She took his hand and they kept walking. "I think we'll live through it." They walked a minute in comfortable silence. One thing she loved about Jesse was how thoughtful he was. He didn't need to fill every silence with words, and neither did she. But that text was weighing on her mind. She squeezed his hand. "Hey, so, a couple of my friends from Jamaica just texted. They're in town and wanted me to meet up with them for dinner tomorrow night. You didn't have anything planned for us, did you?"

"No." He turned his head to the side, eyeing her. "This isn't the famous Todd, is it?"

She was a little surprised he remembered Todd's name. "No. It's a married couple, Ingrid and Noel. They work on the team with us sometimes, get their own team together other times, whatever works for the work."

"Us?" he asked.

She looked at him curiously until she realized what she said. "By *us*, I meant the team I normally work on."

"With Todd?" he asked.

"Why are you so interested in him all of the sudden?" she asked.

"Because, whoever this guy is, I have a feeling he's into you."

If she'd been chewing gum right then, she'd have accidentally gulped it down. "Why would you say that?"

"Because look at you. What guy wouldn't be hot for you? Mix in working in close quarters for two months, and if he's single, a hundred bucks says he's into you. Hell, if he's not single."

She pulled her hair back out of her face, guessing now was as good a time as any to divulge this information. "Well, we actually were together in Jamaica."

"Oh. Damn. I assumed he was into you. I guess I

didn't assume you were into him back. I had such a hard time tearing down your walls, I thought others did, too, but I guess not."

She wasn't sure how to respond to that, so she didn't.

"So, you slept with him," he said, staring out at the ocean. It wasn't a question. "Like just a couple of months ago?"

"Yes."

Color seeped up through his neck. "So, what happened?"

"I made it clear from the start that I wasn't interested in anything serious or taking any ties home with me. He agreed to my terms, but when I left, he sort of put it all on the line for me."

His expression turned sour.

She continued. "He said he loved me and that he wanted me to consider moving there to partner with him full-time, or as much as I wanted, really."

"Did you consider it? Hang on. Are you considering it?"

"I was considering it when I first returned."

He stopped and faced her. "Were you still considering it when we slept together for the first time?" He dropped his posture, glancing around. "God, that wasn't long after you'd slept with him, was it?"

She pointed at him. "Tread lightly here."

He held up two hands, mouth tight, carefully choosing his words. "It's just a lot for me to digest right now. I don't want to think about some other guy having his dick in you this year. And it's only fucking April."

She headed back down the beach, but he grabbed her. "I'm sorry. I didn't mean that."

"You're telling me you haven't had your dick in some other woman since January?"

"Yeah, I am telling you that. Before you, I hadn't done it since like September."

She was definitely surprised to hear that. "Really?"

"Really. I know I have this rep as a player, and I definitely used to be, but I'd gotten sick of it. Why do you think I was so quick on the draw that first night? I was out of practice."

She shook her head, realizing they'd gotten off topic, though this one was an interesting one. "Anyway, so I'm going to text them back about dinner tomorrow night. I just wanted to make sure it didn't interfere with anything you had planned for us."

They started walking back toward the group. "So, it's just these two friends?" he asked.

"Yes, they're a married couple." She wasn't sure why she thought that bore repeating.

"I'd love to meet them," he said.

She slowed, realizing it hadn't even crossed her mind to invite him. What was up with that? "You would?" she asked, a delay tactic while she thought it through.

"Yes, of course I would." He searched her gaze. "But apparently you don't want them to meet me."

"I didn't say that."

"I can see it in your eyes. God, are we back to this, really?"

"We're not back to anything. I'm standing on the

beach with you in a bikini you picked out for me in front of a huge group of my friends, right down the beach."

He stopped. "Don't act like you chose to introduce me to your friends. I've known Dane since college, and the rest of those guys have been coming in the Guppy for years. Bo invited me to his house that night and Chase invited me on the wedding weekend when they were at my bar for cards."

"Okay, fair enough." She let out a resigned sigh. "Of course I would like for my friends from Jamaica to meet you."

"Are you afraid they're going to report back to Todd that you've got a boy toy?"

She hated that he could read her mind. "Not because I'm ashamed of you, but because I don't want to hurt him. Can you understand that?"

He pulled her to him. "Yeah, I can understand it. I still want to kick his ass."

She smiled. "It would not be a fair fight. He's old and not in the greatest of shape."

"I would think he would need to be to do physical labor all the time."

"Todd's more of a supervisor. He's on his feet a lot and active, but he's not driving as many nails into boards as you'd think."

"You mean he's not…ripped?" Jesse grunted as he made fists, posing like a weightlifter.

She took his hand and dragged him into the ocean. "Come on, tough guy. Show me your ocean."

"With pleasure."

Chapter Twenty-One

As Cassidy and Jesse walked through the parking lot, he kept her in his peripheral. She was nervous, he could see that, clearly. She dug around in her purse as they walked, when what he wanted was for her to take his hand and confidently stride into this restaurant with him.

"Hey," he said, when they were still out of sight of the door. "Are you sure about me being here?"

She gave him a resigned smile. "Of course I am." She did better than taking his hand, she took his arm, and he escorted her to the door, making him feel like the king of the goddamned prom.

He opened the door and let her in, and as they glanced around, a woman at a table across the way stood and waved. Cassidy lit up, waving back. She walked quickly to meet the woman who came around from her seat and embraced Cassidy in a hug. But as they were hugging, Jesse couldn't help but notice there were two men at the four-top table.

When Cassidy pulled away from the woman, she went to the man who had been seated next to the woman, and he beamed and kissed her on the cheek. Cassidy pulled away from the guy she was hugging, grabbing his arm and turning to Jesse like she was getting ready to make introductions, but then she caught sight of the other guy.

The guy stood a few inches taller than Jesse, but that was all he had on him in the looks category. He was hanging onto his hair for dear life, and his untucked shirt didn't do enough to hide his beer gut poking out. Jesse didn't know what to think about this. If this was the guy that preceded him, she clearly wasn't into looks. Goddamn, how had Jesse managed to land her? And more importantly, how was he going to keep her?

"Todd," she said with a hard breath. "I didn't realize you were here."

She grabbed Jesse like she was going to introduce them at the same time the guy went for a hug, and Jesse got caught in between their super awkward moment. He stepped back to get out of their way, and they hugged, the guy closing his eyes as he very obviously inhaled a whiff of her hair. Oh, that fucker was going down.

"Wow," Cassidy said, looking completely flushed. She turned to Jesse like she momentarily forgot he was there. "Okay, I um…I need to introduce you."

Jesse couldn't handle hearing her call him a friend or whatever she was getting ready to do, because plan A of just introducing Jesse to a married couple had gone out the window. Plan B of introducing him to her very fresh ex was in motion. He reached for the woman's hand first. "I'm Jesse."

"Ingrid," the woman said, kind, but unsteady.

"Noel," her husband said, sturdier. Jesse got the feeling this guy didn't shock easily.

Jesse turned to Todd and held out a hand, wondering if this guy was old enough to legitimately be his dad. "Jesse Kirby," Jesse said with goddamned authority.

"Todd Packwood," the guy said, his cheeks flushed. Jesse's probably were, too. Cassidy's damn sure were.

When introductions were finished, Jesse noticed that Noel had grabbed a server and was pointing at their table. He came over to them. "I'm so sorry. We're full-up right now, but I can put an extra chair here on the end. Will that work?"

"Of course," Cassidy said.

The server took a spare chair at the table next to theirs and scooted it to their table. "There we go. What can I get the two of you to drink? Would you like to see a wine list?"

"Oh, um," Cassidy uttered, looking flustered. Jesse had never seen Cassidy so stumped. It was starting to really worry him.

He took her arm to calm her. "I'm driving so I'm just gonna get a light beer. Do you want a glass of Chardonnay?"

She nodded, her face flooded red. "That'd be perfect."

The server asked her if the house brand was okay, and she nodded. "What kind of beer for you, sir?"

"Whatever light beer you have on tap is fine. Thanks."

The server left, and they stood there awkwardly looking down at the seating arrangements. As much as Jesse wanted to plant his ass right there between Cassidy and this Todd guy, he wasn't going to make his girl sit on the end. He pulled the chair back for her. "You sit here. I'll sit on the end."

"Oh, I can…" Cassidy said, seeming like she was trying to make sense of the chair.

"No, please. Sit."

She did, and he scooted her toward the table. The Todd guy seated himself, his confusion about who Jesse was to Cassidy clearing up and showing in his face. Good.

"So, Jesse," Ingrid said. "How do you know Cassidy?"

He looked at Cassidy, wondering how she wanted him to answer the question. When she just sat there with her mouth hanging open, he decided he'd had enough of this shit. "I guess officially we met on business. Her friend Marigold introduced us in hopes that I'd buy cookies from her for my menu. I have a bar in Grayton called the Bohemian Guppy."

Ingrid grabbed Noel's arm. "Didn't someone recommend Grayton to us just this morning? I swear they mentioned that place. Did I dream that?"

"No, I remember the name. Hard to forget," Noel said with a smile. Jesse understood why Cassidy liked these two so much. They were both kind, even in an awkward situation. "So you two work together, in a way?" Noel asked, glancing between Jesse and Cassidy.

He waited for Cassidy to speak up, but she just sort of smiled, looking anywhere but at Todd, who was watching her like a hawk. "So, how did the meeting with the donor go?" Cassidy asked, glancing at all three of them and then focusing on Ingrid, which was clearly her safe place.

"It went well. With some finessing from Todd, I think we're going to be able to do another project in July. We know that's the hottest month there, but it's also got the least amount of rain, so if we dig in, we can do a lot before the rainy season kicks back in."

"Sounds like you've got it figured out. I know you've done a lot of these," Jesse said.

As Ingrid talked about some of the past work they'd done, the tension between Cassidy and Todd was becoming palpable. Jesse tried his hardest to pay attention to Ingrid and Noel and kept asking questions about the work to keep them talking. When that was done, he asked where they were from and what work they did when they weren't in Jamaica, and anything else he could think of to keep the conversation going. Cassidy's silence filled Jesse's gut with nothingness, and he questioned everything they'd had before they'd walked into this godforsaken place.

After they ate and finished off another bottle of wine, the server came over. "How should I split this?"

While Todd and Noel were arguing over who to give the bill to, Jesse pulled his credit card out of his wallet and handed it to the server, who was gone before anyone could protest.

Noel smiled at him. "That was smooth. I'll have

to remember that trick."

"You'd have to give up getting to scour the bill for errors," Ingrid said.

"Well, that's true. I'd lose sleep for a week trying to figure out how I got screwed out of a quarter."

Todd shifted uncomfortably in his chair. "Thanks, but I really did want to pay."

"Yes," Ingrid said, "thank you so much Jesse, and Cassidy?" she said the last part of the sentence like a question.

"It's our pleasure," Jesse said, looking at Cassidy. She smiled at him, but it didn't reach her eyes.

Todd scratched his forehead. "Um, would you mind if I stole her away for a moment?"

Jesse's blood went hot. "No problem."

Todd and Cassidy both stood, and he put his hand on the small of her back for a brief moment as he led her toward the outside deck. The idea that this man was comfortable touching her possessively like that made Jesse's skin crawl.

Jesse turned back to Ingrid and Noel, who both just smiled at him awkwardly. They met each other's gaze thoughtfully, and then they turned back to Jesse. Ingrid put her hand down flat on the table. "I'm so sorry if we ambushed you here. It was clear on Cassidy's face she didn't know Todd was coming. I hope this evening hasn't been unbearable."

Jesse shook his head. "Not at all. I've really enjoyed getting to know both of you."

"The pleasure has been all ours, Jesse," Noel said with a reassuring nod. "I'm not sure where you two are in the scheme of things, but I wish you both happiness."

Jesse smiled. "That's very kind. Thanks."

Ingrid smiled, nodding, and then they all shifted their gaze to the door to the back deck.

Cassidy stood at the back of the deck area, elbow resting on the railing, wishing she was anywhere on earth than in this position. She'd failed miserably the entire night. Why hadn't she thought to ask Ingrid if the *we* had just meant her and Noel? But then Cassidy had figured if Todd had been in town he would have been the one to contact her. It felt like a sabotage, though she really didn't want to believe that was the case.

To Jesse's credit, he'd performed like a champ. He was gracious, polite, kind, engaging...she couldn't possibly have asked for him to do anything differently or better. She, on the other hand, had blown the entire evening. She'd chosen to flounder between the two men, so afraid of hurting Todd, who didn't deserve to have Jesse thrown up in his face, making him feel like a fifth wheel on a blind date with the woman he'd professed his love to a couple of months ago.

"So, I take it Ingrid and Noel hadn't mentioned I was coming," Todd started.

"It never occurred to me to ask. I just assumed the donor she was referring to was someone for a project they were putting together."

He nodded, messing with a splinter of wood in the railing. "Jesse seems very nice."

"Yes, he's wonderful," she said, trying to straddle the fence between being fair to Jesse and not throwing him in Todd's face.

Todd's expression turned sour, and then a rueful smile crossed his face. "I just...wow, Cassidy."

Her defenses flew up. "Excuse me?"

"I'm sorry, but I've just got to ask. How old is he?"

"That's none of your goddamned business," she said, using a word she saved for particular indignant moments.

"No, you're right. It's not. But this is just so out of character for you."

"Dating a wonderful man?" she asked, both making a point and driving a screw in. She couldn't help it. He was attacking the man she loved.

"You can't have been with him long. You were just with me in February."

She chose not to respond to that.

"I'm just surprised you would bring him to a dinner with Ingrid and Noel."

"Why is that surprising?"

"Because you're intensely private. You've never introduced anyone you've been dating to any of us. But you chose this guy to start with? Two months after you split up with me?"

"First of all, I didn't split up with you, Todd. I told you from the start I didn't want anything serious. I thought we were having a good time."

"Well, I wasn't."

She stepped back eyebrows up.

He shook his head. "I didn't mean it like that. I took the deal because I was desperate to be with you. I've been in love with you for years now."

"That's not possible, Todd. You've not spent enough time with me over the years to be in love with me. Besides, you've been with other women since we've known one another."

"Because I'd expressed interest in you and you'd blown me off. When I kissed you that night at the camp, I couldn't believe you let me. I would have sold my soul to the devil to have been with you. Of course I was going to agree to keep it casual."

"I never knew your feelings were that strong. I never would have slept with you had I known."

"Well, now you know. So this is it? This guy is the one?"

She averted her gaze to the ocean.

He gripped the railing glancing around. "God, I just don't see it."

"What don't you see, Todd?"

"He's not a long-term solution."

She huffed a laugh. "Well, he's not a roof or a used car part, so…"

"He's temporary. Can you not see that?"

The words stung her like she'd been hit by a lightning bolt. "You better watch it, Todd."

"He is. I'm sorry. But you've apparently been blinded by his abs and his goddamned tattoos. Really, Cassidy? Tattoos?"

She started to walk away but he grabbed her arm. "I'm sorry. That was unfair. But you need to hear this. If nobody else in your life is brave enough to tell you this, then I'm going to. Look, I get that this must be thrilling for you to be able to relive your twenties or whatever through this guy. But when the newness has worn off, he's not going to stick around, and he's going to leave you feeling like a fool. Life isn't about lust, Cassidy. It's about serving others. It's about people's hearts and souls."

The idea of Todd standing there lecturing her about life was more than her restraint could handle. "Is it, Todd? Is that what life is about? People's hearts and souls? I'm just curious then. What exactly made you fall in love with me? Was it my big heart? Was it the fact that I love to bake cupcakes and sit on the front porch of my beach house in privileged Seaside, Florida when I'm not by your side in Jamaica painting or learning carpentry while you walk around *supervising*?" She put air quotes around that last word. "Was it my heart that you fell in love with, or was it my...what did you call it...body like Heidi Klum's?"

He scratched his forehead, lips puckered into a tight wad.

She looked heavenward like she was trying to remember something. "'I've never gotten to make love to a body like yours,' was another killer line that just really fed my need to be respected and taken seriously intellectually."

He held both hands up. "Okay, so fucking sue me for enjoying your body."

"Then don't sue me for enjoying his." She knew it was the wrong thing to say the second it left her mouth. It reduced Jesse to a toy and supported everything Todd was saying.

Fueled with her slip-up, Todd's eyes gleamed. "Where do you think this is going with him? Does he want to have kids? Is that an option for you?" he asked, brows furrowed like she was being ridiculous.

He'd punched her in the gut, temporarily taking away her ability to retort.

"I get why he's with you now. You're beautiful. But what's going to happen in ten years? Fifteen? Twenty? You're not going to look like this. You're going to age, and he will too, but do you think when you're fifty-five or sixty, and you're dealing with inevitable health issues that come with aging that he's going to be as gung-ho about you then? Do you seriously believe that this bartender, this tattooed surfer guy is going to be by your side during your time of crisis…your time of need like I would?"

The pressure building behind her eyes threatened to get the best of her, but she refused to let it. She smiled, swiping at a tear that had escaped. "Yes, Todd. I do believe that."

He snickered, moving his hand over his balding head, smoothing back a clump of stray hair that had served as a form of a comb-over. "Well, if nobody else will say it, then I will. You look foolish."

She smiled and shouldered her purse. "No, Todd. You're the only fool here." She turned and walked away, and this time he didn't try to stop her.

When she got to the table, Noel, Ingrid, and Jesse stood with looks of sincere concern on their faces. Cassidy remembered that she was horrible at hiding her emotions, and God knew she probably looked like a wreck right then. She put her arms around Ingrid. "It was so lovely to catch up with you."

"Yes, I'm so glad we got to do this."

She hugged Noel next. "So good to see you."

"Never lasts long enough," Noel said.

She turned to Jesse, reaching behind his head and pulled him to her for a kiss. She smiled at him. "Let's go home."

She waved at Ingrid and Noel, who stood a little dumbfounded, and hated that this would probably be the last time she saw them…at least as long as they were working with Todd.

Chapter Twenty-Two

Cassidy was quiet the whole way back to her house from Miramar, staring out the window and biting on her thumbnail. Jesse turned on the radio to fill the emptiness between them, but what he really wanted was to know why she had that frown on her face and what it meant for them.

He pulled into the driveway and cut off the engine. She opened the door, but when he did not, she hesitated and then closed the door. "You're not coming in," she stated rather than asked.

"I'm not sure if I'm welcome to."

She let her head fall to the side like she was so exhausted she could barely keep her eyes open. "Jesse."

"I'm serious, Cassidy. What happened back there?"

She shook her head, looking out the window.

Acid churned in his stomach. "What did he say to

you?" he asked, each word deliberate.

She met his gaze. "Nothing I hadn't already been running through my head a hundred times a day."

He turned his body to face her, waiting.

She stared at him hard. "Do you want to know why I don't like to be on top? It's because I don't want you to see just how cruel gravity is to a forty-four-year-old woman's breasts. I also don't want you behind me in bed because the thought of you getting an up close and personal view of the saggy skin on the backs of my thighs makes me worried that you're going to realize that I'm a middle-aged lady." She pressed her hand against her forehead. "I know I look good right now, thanks to my father's side of the family, but I'm going to be fifty in six years. Fifty years old. And you'll be thirty-five. You've worn sunscreen out of the house every day since you were a kid. You're going to age like George freaking Clooney. I just spent two months in Jamaica where sunscreen was the last of my priorities. I know you say you're crazy about me, and you're attracted to me, but I'm hanging on to what's left of my youth by a shoestring. You're just getting started with yours." She pinched the bridge of her nose. "I thought I could do this. I thought, 'We're not talking about forever. We're talking about for now,' and that's how I've been operating all this time. You would tire of me or realize the gimmick had worn off, and we'd call this a day, and I would get back to my real life. But I've slid so far down into this place with you, that if I don't find a way out now..." She shook her head, looking back out the window.

He sat there thinking of all the times he'd

reassured her about their differences, wondering if there would ever be a way to make her see sense. "I love you, Cassidy, and it has nothing to do with your body. Sure, your looks were what drew me to you a hundred percent. I won't lie about that. And I wanted in your pants. I wanted to lay this hot, sophisticated woman who intrigued the hell out of me. Then I did, way faster than I thought I would, but even then, I was fucking hooked. I fell for your heart. I loved that you'd done all these amazing things but were completely self-effacing about it. You have this uncanny ability to ask all the right questions but not to push when you see something off. You're by far the kindest and most considerate person I've ever known." He swallowed hard, his throat welling up. "You're more of a family to me than my own family has ever been. I fall more in love with you every day, every goddamned moment. So the idea that you think that I would consider letting you leave my life over saggy boobs or skin on the back of your legs makes me realize that I've fucked up epically in expressing to you exactly why I'm so in love with you." He took her quivering hand in his own. "I'm madly in love with your heart and your mind. I have zero fucks to give about your body."

She huffed a laugh that sort of went into a sob. Holding her hand over her mouth, she steadied and calmed herself, swallowing hard and then sitting up straight, closing her eyes. After a moment, she opened them and shouldered the strap on her purse. "I have never, nor will I ever, love a man as much as I have loved you." She squeezed his hand, let go, and then got out of the car and went inside without him.

Chapter Twenty-Three

Jesse lay slumped on the couch on his fifth episode of *The Love Boat*. It'd been a week since Cassidy walked away from him, and with every day that passed, he sank deeper into misery. When he'd found out his brother had been sleeping with his girlfriend, he was filled with rage for years. He'd kill for rage right now, because it would mean he was alive.

For weeks since he'd told Cassidy he loved her, he'd been patiently waiting for her to say it back. He'd have given her a lifetime to say it, just as long as he could be with her. But when she finally did say it, she dropped the bomb on him and walked away, the implication clearly being not to follow.

Whatever that asshole had said to her back at that restaurant had changed her mind about everything they had. Jesse couldn't help blaming him, though he knew his anger was misdirected. Whatever Cassidy had in her head about their age difference was there whether that guy cemented it or not. But it didn't stop him from wanting to dismember the guy.

The door to Gracie's room opened and she came out wearing pajama pants and a long T-shirt. Well, long for her, normal for anyone else. She messed around in the kitchen and then walked over to the couch and handed him a bowl.

"I don't want anything."

"You need to eat. You look sickly."

"I'm fine."

"You're going to get skinny, and nobody wants a skinny guy."

He glanced over at her shoulder. "Are you wearing a bra?"

"I'm being respectful. I've been dressing like this for a month now at home, in case you didn't notice." He shifted in his seat, and she shoved the bowl at him. "Eat."

"What is it?"

"Homemade trail mix. I dried the fruit myself."

"Really?"

"No, dumbass. Just eat it. It's good. All natural. Local honey."

He tried to eat a mouthful, but his body was rejecting food. "It's good," he said as he set it down on the table.

"Man, this woman did a number on you, didn't she?"

"It's not her fault," he said, his defenses up.

She chuckled. "My God. A woman breaks up with you, devastating you to the point of *The Love Boat*, and you take up for her? You've lost your mind."

"She's got it in her head somehow that I'm going

to fall out of love with her when she loses her looks."

"Women are insecure about these things."

"But not her. Not usually. She's more comfortable in her own skin than anyone I've ever known."

"Love does this shit to people. It makes you super-vulnerable. I met that woman, and I saw her a few times at the bar. That's not a woman who's used to losing control." She set her bowl down on the coffee table. "Not that you need a bigger head than the one you've already got, but you're one of the hottest guys I've ever known. You're probably the hottest guy she's dated in a while, maybe ever. She's scared. She can't control the fact that she's aging, and she's scared shitless about it." She held her arms out to her sides. "Look at me." I'm freaked out because I'm getting ready to be twenty-four, and that puts me one step closer to twenty-five. I'm terrified about turning twenty-five."

"Why?"

"Because that means no more excuses. You can only claim youth for your fuck-ups for so long, and my clock is ticking."

"You've got your life together though," Jesse said.

"Not really. I'm still mooching off my best friend, which I know I need to fix. I'm working on it. But anyway, we're getting off topic. Just cut her some slack for this. She's processing through some shit. Give her some time to work it out."

An ugly desperation crawled up his spine. "I don't know if I have time. This idiot guy wants her to come to Jamaica with him permanently. He's been trying to get her to do that since January. What if she decides to?"

She pursed her lips at him, considering. "Did you ever patch things up with your sister?"

"No. Why?"

"She was a bitch to Cassidy, wasn't she? She said some shit to her, too, about being old, didn't she?"

He forgot he'd told her about that. He'd been stewing about it that day when he'd come to the bar and seen her. He hadn't told Gracie about the miscarriage, of course, but he'd told her Rachel was shitty to Cassidy. "Yeah."

"You need to get your sister to welcome her to your family."

He gave a humorless laugh. "You don't know my sister."

"How desperate are you to win this girl back?"

He turned to her. "Pretty goddamned desperate."

She motioned at him like *there you go*.

"Why would that help?"

"Because Rachel is like your mom to you. If Cassidy gets a stamp of approval from her it may help."

"What if it doesn't?"

"Then we'll formulate Plan B."

He smiled at her. "I never knew you were such a problem-solver."

"You haven't had many problems to solve since I've known you. I've been waiting on my moment to shine all this time. Seriously, I'm happy to pay you back for all you've done for me."

He considered her. "Thanks."

She picked up the bowl from the coffee table. "Now eat."

"Later," he said. "I've got a flight to book."

Chapter Twenty-Four

As Jesse parked the rental car in his sister's driveway, his bravado wavered a bit. He'd been so desperate to fix this problem with Cassidy that anything he had to do to get her back was palatable, even a conversation with his sister. But now that he was getting ready to face her, the weight of the task ahead bore down on his shoulders.

He headed up the walk, flipping the car key around his finger. He didn't even know if Rachel was home. There was a car in the driveway, but he'd never paid attention to what she drove the one time a year he came to see her. He checked his phone for the time. Five forty. She was probably making dinner, and she definitely wasn't expecting him. He hadn't warned her he was coming, not sure what he was going to say yet.

Collecting his breath, and his courage, he knocked on the door. After a moment, it opened.

Rachel blinked. "Wow. What's going on here?" She glanced around him.

"I'm alone," he said. He hated how visibly relieved that statement made her.

She opened the door. "Come on in. I was just deciding if I was going to cook dinner or not. I'm seriously considering ordering pizza. I would if I hadn't already ordered it another time this week."

He was sort of shocked to hear it. "You let your kids eat pizza more than once a week?"

She pulled a chair at her kitchen table back to sit. "I let my kids do a lot these days. I'm exhausted."

He narrowed his gaze, wondering if she was pregnant again. She'd been tired through all three of her pregnancies. "You...okay?"

She waved him off. "I'm fine. Just mentally tired. It's been a year."

Jesse sat down, wondering if he was contributing to his sister's physical and mental health issues. "How's Justin?" Seeing him in person had somehow made it easier to say his name aloud.

"Sober, at least for now. Lauren made him join AA. She threatened to kick him out if he didn't try to straighten up his attitude."

"By the way he was talking, that sounded like his dream come true."

"You know Justin. He was just whining. He'd never actually leave her."

Jesse nodded, looking out the window, realizing he didn't know his brother at all, not anymore. He narrowed his gaze at the backyard. "Are the kids somewhere?"

"Next door neighbor's house. They've got two

boys. I trade off with their mom. She takes them one afternoon and I'll take them the next. It's hell when you're on duty, but then when you're off, it's bliss. I should be using the time to make some kind of healthy dinner, but you see what I had pulled up on my phone before you rang the bell." She held up her phone to him which had a pizza menu on it.

"You don't cook healthy meals full of steamed vegetables for your kids every night?"

She pointed at him with her phone. "You're thinking of the old Rachel."

He blew a puff of air out his nose. "I guess I don't know either of you like I used to."

"Can't imagine how that happened," she said, eyebrows raised.

Jesse messed with the placemat in front of him. "I didn't know he was struggling with drinking. How long has that been going on?"

Rachel shrugged. "It's hard to say. He's always been a drinker. It's been more noticeable since they had the baby…well, actually, further back than that. Lauren quit as soon as she got pregnant, of course. Chuck and I don't drink as much as we used to. Someone's got to be sober in case one of these kids falls out of a tree or something. Pete drinks but he and Mom aren't around as much as they used to be."

"Is that okay with you…with the kids and all?"

She shrugged. "It's nothing new. She wasn't around much for us. I never had illusions she'd be around for my kids."

Jesse considered his sister who'd been old for as long as he could remember. She seemed ten years older than Cassidy, but it was the other way around.

A shock of anger came over him as he remembered her telling Cassidy about the miscarriage, but he wasn't here to deepen their divide, so he calmed his emotions before speaking. "I wish you wouldn't have told Cassidy about the miscarriage. That should have been my choice."

She nodded, looking at least a little contrite. "I know. It was wrong of me. But I was desperate."

"For what?"

"To help you. Look, she seems like a lovely person, and if she had something to do with getting you to see Justin again, then I'm truly grateful for her. But I can't sit by and let you partner up with a woman who's double your age."

He let his head fall to the side. "Rachel."

"Well, close enough. She's got to be forty, right? Getting pregnant at forty is not easy. It takes fertility drugs lots of times and there are high risks at that age, and—"

"Why would you assume she's trying to get pregnant?"

Rachel blinked. "Because. You've always wanted to have kids."

"No I haven't."

"You cried like a baby when Lauren had that miscarriage."

He closed his eyes, stilling himself, and then opened them once he'd calmed. "Rachel, that was a very different time in my life. I was a different person. I was a fucking accountant, for crissakes. Look at me." He held his arms out to the sides. "I'm not that person anymore."

"Well, maybe that's what scares me, Jesse."

It was his turn to be shocked. "What does that mean?"

She sat back in her chair, gauging him. "Think about this from my viewpoint. My little brother is this nerdy little library geek who reads incessantly and goes to college to study accounting. You meet this sweet, wholesome girl whose father takes you under his wing and grooms you to be this corporate bigwig." She wiped her hands together. "My work is done here. One less brother to worry about. Then when it all goes to hell, you lose your shit. You move to freaking Florida where I can't be anywhere near you to help you out. You don't share any info with me anymore. Hell, you don't even talk to me. You get all tatted up and buy this bar and live in it."

"Above it."

"Same freaking difference." She tossed a hand at him. "I don't even know who you are anymore. Then the first woman you bring to meet me is forty."

He didn't dare correct the age she had in her head.

"I just—" She stopped herself, staring at him like she wanted to say something, and he had an idea what it was.

"Go ahead," he said.

"Do you even know who you are?"

He had been expecting her to say he was living out some kind of missing mother complex or syndrome or something. This question took him off guard.

"What does that mean?"

She took a pair of glasses off the top of her head and set them on the table, leaning in. "It means you were someone for many years, and then you became

231

this person out of spite or anger or just wanting to be as opposite of your old life as possible. I get it. But who is the real Jesse? Have you figured that out?"

He swallowed hard, both hating and appreciating his sister's uncanny ability to cut deeper into him than anyone on the planet. "What does that even fucking mean? Who am I? I'm fucking me. That's a stupid thing to ask." He was trying to undercut her point…trivialize it. That way he wouldn't have to think too hard about it.

All she did was stare at him, and the shame within him grew. He shifted in his seat.

He finally met her gaze. "I love Cassidy. She is the reason I agreed to see Justin. She grounds me in a way I never knew was possible. She loves me and puts my needs before her own. She's sweet and compassionate and one of the most kind-hearted people I've ever known. She spends her winters in Jamaica helping people, building schools and stuff. She's freaking amazing." He met her gaze. "I want you to know that. I want you to know her. I want you to accept her."

Rachel sat back, picking up her phone and tapping it on the table absentmindedly as she stared at him. "If this woman is truly the person you want to be with, then I'll accept her with my whole heart. All I ask is that you love yourself before you love her."

A chill shot down Jesse's spine, and he wasn't sure if he could speak. Rachel picked up her phone and headed out to the deck, shutting the door behind her and leaving him with nothing but his own jumbled thoughts.

Chapter Twenty-Five

Cassidy stood in front of the workspace in the Seaside Sweets kitchen, staring at a recipe. She knew leaving Jesse would be hard, but she hadn't dreamed of the enormity of this blanket of depression that covered her. It was tough now but would pay off later, she kept reminding herself. Jesse deserved a woman his own age. He deserved a family and a beautiful, young wife. Cassidy and he had fallen into the middle of something ridiculously intense. They'd gotten wrapped up in each other in a way Cassidy had never known, and it had scared the hell out of her.

Time would heal this unbearable emptiness inside of her, she was sure of that. Now that he'd seen his brother and his ex and had some closure there, he could move on. Lovely young women his own age came into his bar every night. He'd meet one and they'd fall in love. Now that he was free of the monkey on his back, this was the next logical step. It was time for Cassidy to step aside and let that happen.

The double doors swung open, waking Cassidy from her trance. "We've got visitors," Marigold sang.

Cassidy wiped off her hands that weren't even dirty yet and headed out there. Tears welled up behind her eyes when she saw Seanna and Sebastian standing side by side. "What are you two doing here together?" she asked, swiping at her eyes, trying not to make a fool of herself.

"Reinforcements have been called in," Sebastian said. "Get your purse. We're having a spa day."

She let the tension drop out of her shoulders. "Oh, guys, that is so sweet of you. But I can't. We're still on the tail end of spring break. It was slammed in here up until about a half hour ago. I can't leave Marigold."

On cue, Marigold tossed Seanna an apron, and she said. "That's what I'm here for."

Cassidy blinked. "But you've got to work."

"It's Saturday."

She looked at Marigold for confirmation, and she nodded.

"No, sweetie. I'm not letting you work here on your day off."

"Blake's at the clinic. Besides, I'm looking forward to it. I haven't hung with Marigold solo in months. I still need to know more about this Dane guy who's been taking up all her time."

Sebastian tossed up both hands. "You're stuck with me."

Seanna tied her apron around her waist, surveying

the workspace behind the counter. "Yep, pretty much looks identical to when I worked here. I think we're good." She nodded at Marigold.

"Yep," Marigold said, handing Cassidy her purse. When had she gotten that?

Sebastian came around the counter and took Cassidy's hand. "So now, all you have to do is walk with me, right this way, pretty lady, so we aren't late for our appointment."

"What do we have an appointment for?" Cassidy asked.

"Pedicures and therapy, both on me."

Cassidy would continue to argue but she literally did not have the strength.

When Cassidy's nail tech got her settled under a dryer, Sebastian dropped his magazine and came over to sit next to her. "Let me see the color. Pretty in pink. I love it."

She turned to him, her body feeling drained of energy. "Thank you."

"You're welcome, hon. Now let's get down to business."

Cassidy let out an exhaustive sigh. "I love you for doing this for me, Sebastian, but I can't talk about it."

"Oh, you can and you will. Marigold is worried about you, and therefore we're all worried. Right now it's just Seanna and me who she's called, but she will not stop until our whole group is crowded around you with pillows and cups of herbal tea. So either you talk to me about this now, or you pay later."

She bit her lip, relaxing back on the pillow behind

her. "It's nothing, honestly. I just needed to end things before they got too heavy."

"Mmm hmm, because you staring into space for a week solid isn't heavy at all. What happened here, sweetie?"

Hoping to even temporarily lift the crushing burden of sorrow, she told Sebastian about the dinner and the talk with Todd on the deck.

"Mmm-kay. He seems lovely. Tell me again why you let this pompous asshole influence you?"

"Because he said everything I'd already been thinking. I know that Jesse thinks he loves me now, but—"

"*Thinks* he loves you?"

"Okay, does love me now, and truth be known, he would probably love me forever if I let him. But how can I let him? How can I selfishly take this man's love and keep him from having a traditional family with kids and grandkids and all of that stuff?"

"He wants kids and grandkids?"

"Not right this minute, but even he admitted he doesn't know how he'll feel in five years."

"So be with him five years then reevaluate."

"So I'm supposed to build a life with him that has this ticking clock on it? A bomb sitting out there waiting to go off at any minute. We'll be walking down the beach in a few years and a little boy and girl will run out in front of us, and he'll be looking at them longingly, and then I'll be like, *okay, today's the day it's happening*. I can't live like that."

"Okay, woman, you are scaring me."

She looked up at him. "What?"

"You're creating imaginary scenarios that are

never even going to happen."

"You don't know that," she said, completely unreasonably.

"Well, I do know this. From all you've told me about him, and from all I've witnessed, including our group falling head over heels for him, he's fabulous. Maybe it's okay if this life of yours together *is* the wonderful thing for the both of you. Maybe it's a life filled with love and leisurely mornings with coffee and late nights out on the town or uninterrupted in bed. That's okay. Just because you're a straight couple, you're not required to have children."

"I hear you, but I can't get around the feeling that being with him is selfish on my part. I feel like I'm taking something away from him, and all I want is to give him everything on this earth."

Sebastian laughed, shaking his head at her.

"What?"

He motioned at her. "Are you hearing yourself? All you want is to give him everything. This is love, Cassidy. Love. When have you ever felt it like this?"

She closed her eyes, the pressure mounting in her chest and throat, because she'd never felt like this, never in her adult dating life, not even close. She shook her head.

"And what about him? Do you think he's ever felt this way before?"

She thought about all he'd said to her, the sincerity in his words, how she'd brought light into his darkness and years of fucking around with women. She shook her head, the pain of the loss of this beautiful man starting to rip into her from the inside out.

Sebastian took her hand. "This is it, sweetie. This is the great love of your lives. You've found one another. Congratulations. So many of us haven't and may never."

She met Sebastian's gaze thinking she wasn't sure how much more pain her heart could hold. She'd found what he'd been searching for all these years, and she was throwing it away.

She squeezed his hand, hard. "You will find him."

Sebastian's eyes went glassy. "Of course I will, sweetie. But when I do, I can promise you I won't throw him back. I will thank my lucky stars that our paths crossed, and I will hold onto him for dear life."

Tears streamed down her face. She'd never cried so much in her life, but she was a damn waterfall these days. Sebastian handed her his handkerchief. The fact that he carried one alone surely was enough to merit a wonderful soulmate for him.

She met his gaze. "I'm not sure I'll ever be able to earn the friendship you give me."

He waved her off. "Just make sure to keep saving me a place at your Thanksgiving table and we're golden."

She pulled him in for a hug. "You're my family. There'll always be a place for you at my table."

He grabbed the handkerchief back from her and dabbed his eyes. "Oh, stop it. You'll ruin my mascara."

She giggled, and then brought him in to her again, kissing him on the top of the head.

Cassidy's whole body emanated a buzz as she walked toward Jesse's bar. While she still wasn't convinced she was doing the right thing, she had decided she'd let herself continue to fall in love with him, come what may. If he left her in a few years, then so be it. And since when did she worry about more than the day in front of her? Since she'd fallen madly in love and lost all sense. That was when.

She blew out a deep breath, ready to see him and tell him what a mistake she'd made. She'd explain how while it felt like she'd been doing it for him so that he could be free to move forward and meet someone else, that in reality, it was because she had been afraid. And while she was still terrified, she understood that was what love did to a person, and it was the risk she had to take.

She opened the door and glanced around the bar, her heart pounding in her chest. She couldn't find him anywhere, but Kelly spotted her at the door and came over with a confused look on her face. "I thought we were okay on cookies for today?"

"Actually, I'm looking for Jesse."

A young woman who looked familiar sidled up next to Kelly. "I got this."

"Gracie," Cassidy said. She supposed she'd spent so much time looking at the young woman's breasts that day in Jesse's apartment that she'd not gotten a good enough look at her face, but her nametag gave her away.

She let out an exhausted sigh, balancing an empty tray on her hand. "Cassidy."

Cassidy swallowed, feeling like this girl's junior. "I'm actually glad I'm seeing you, Gracie. I meant to have done this already. I apologize for the way I acted when I saw you that day in Jess—" She cut herself off before finishing, "your apartment. You were kind to me, and I believe I probably came off as rude. I'm so sorry about that. I was just thrown off. But that really isn't an excuse."

She shrugged. "You seemed fine to me."

Cassidy breathed a sigh of relief. "Well, thank you for saying that, but the apology stands. I'm looking for Jesse, is he here?"

"Jesse's gone."

Cassidy blinked, not understanding what that meant.

"He's in Puerto Rico. A mission trip or something. I'm helping Kelly manage the bar while he's gone."

Cassidy felt like she needed to hang onto something. Luckily the host podium was there. "A trip?"

"Yeah. He's gonna be gone a while. He's supposed to be back like mid to late June?" she said in the form of a question. "Kelly!" she shouted across the bar. "When's Jesse back?"

"June 23," was Kelly's response.

She turned back to Cassidy. "There you go. He's got his phone though, so you can text him if you want. We're trying not to bother him though," she said, pointedly.

Cassidy understood her need to protect him. "Well, I'll have that same respect," she said, a frog climbing her throat.

Gracie pulled her tray in to her chest. "He needs this time, okay? He's going through a lot with his family right now and figuring stuff out. I think he's sort of having a mid-life crisis."

Cassidy bit back the chuckle that wanted to come out from her turn of phrase, because she did understand the point Gracie was trying to put across. "I get it. I'll back off."

"Jesse's an amazing guy. There's been a lot of girls who have come through this bar trying to get with him, and you did, but you let him go, which quite honestly astonishes me, but whatever. You did something for him though. He's getting off his ass and doing something about his life. He's trying to give it some meaning, which is like seriously cool. I'm guessing you had a part in that, so thank you."

Cassidy shook her head, the pressure building behind her eyes again. "That's all him."

"Well, whatever. I gotta get back to my tables." Gracie looked Cassidy up and down. "You're not going to tell me your workout?"

"Oh," Cassidy said, looking down at her body. "Quite honestly, I'm on my feet all day at the bakery. I just collapse when I get home."

Gracie rolled her eyes. "I knew you were a bitch," she said with a little smile, and then headed off.

Cassidy huffed a laugh, and then headed out the door. As she walked to her car, the reality sank in that Jesse was gone till June 23, which was more than two months away. So much could happen in two months. That was more time than it'd taken for her to fall in love with him.

Noel and Ingrid worked with a group out of Puerto Rico sometimes. They'd talked about it that night at dinner. She wondered if Jesse had gotten in touch with them. It wouldn't be hard to reach them with their web and social media presences.

Cassidy rested against the hood of her car in the beach access parking lot, imagining Jesse in Puerto Rico working with a volunteer group. She knew how easy it was to get close with others in those situations, and most of the time, the people who did this kind of work were good-hearted people you wanted to get to know. And God knew people would want to get to know Jesse.

She closed her eyes, letting the realization that she'd let him go sicken her once again. This was what she'd wanted for him—the opportunity to find some good, young woman to build a life with. Maybe he'd do that. Maybe she'd get her wish.

She glanced out at the beach and all the vacationers down there...the families building sand castles, the young couples in love. She spotted something that got her attention, and her feet moved toward it. As she got to the beach, she pulled off her sandals and headed over to the hut and the twenty-something guy manning it. "Is there such a thing as paddleboarding lessons?"

Chapter Twenty-Six

Marigold set a pan of cranberry walnut muffins in the case. "Well, what's the verdict?"

"On?" Cassidy asked, adding a roll of quarters to the register.

"What you're going to wear."

Cassidy smiled as a nervous bug ate away at her stomach. "I haven't really thought about it."

"I call B.S."

She rested against the counter. "I'm trying so hard not to make a big deal of this."

"It is a big deal. Jesse's coming home."

"I'm not even sure I should be there, to be honest."

"Everyone you know will be there. I'll be there. And Sebastian, and Seanna, Blake, Chase, Shayla, Bo—"

"I know. But what if he's bitter toward me for breaking up with him? Or even worse, what if he's completely over it and barely even remembers why he was into me? I haven't spoken a word to this man in over two months. Not a text, nothing." She shut the register, gripping onto the closed drawer. "What if he's brought someone home with him?"

"Let's not get carried away. There's only one scenario going on right now, and it's the unknown one. But regardless of what's happening with him and what's getting ready to happen when we see him tonight, you need to look fabulous."

Cassidy rested against the counter and covered her face. "I don't know if I can do this. It's been two months since I even spoke a word to this man after I broke up with him, and I'm acting like I still have some kind of right to him."

Marigold took her wrists. "You have the right to change your mind."

"And he has the right to tell me to screw off."

"While this is true, he also has the right to forgive and move forward. So let's stop analyzing and start putting together an outfit. Can we please close now?"

"We should have taken an Urban Ride," Sebastian said, circling again for a parking place.

The more they circled, the sicker Cassidy felt. "We could just go home?"

Sebastian let out a big fake laugh that went directly into a glare. "No. Yes!" he shouted as a car came out of a space. "And right out front. Persistence is prudent."

After they parked, Sebastian opened the door, but Cassidy didn't. He shut the door back. "It's gonna be what it's gonna be. But you'll never know until you step inside."

"It's flippant of me to just casually walk in here like I'm welcome."

"Um, didn't you help plan this party basically?"

"I gave Gracie the numbers of all our friends and provided some desserts. That's hardly planning the party."

"Well, regardless, you are welcome. What will it say if you don't show? It's been two months since you broke it off with him. At this point, you'd just look rude for not coming."

She gave him a look.

"Seriously, get your happy ass out of the car, okay? Let's do this thing."

She opened the door, heart up in her throat as they walked toward the pulsing bar. The place was packed with wall-to-wall people, and a band was setting up on the little stage in the far right corner. The first person to greet her was Chase with his big open arms. "Cassidy, long time no see. Where have you been?"

"Oh, at the shop, as usual. How are you?"

Shayla came in with a side hug. "I've missed you, friend."

"I've missed the both of you." Cassidy had been absent from the group's last few functions. She hated to fall into old patterns, but she hadn't had the energy to do much of anything, preferring to stay home on her sofa and stress about what was happening in Puerto Rico. She scratched her neck. "Um, has anyone seen Jesse yet?"

"Rumor has it his flight got delayed," Chase said.

Maya appeared next looking a bit stressed, but that wasn't completely unusual for her. "Hey," she said, hugging Cassidy, and then she tugged on another woman's arm who faced Cassidy. "Do you remember my sister, Meade?"

"Of course. We met at the wedding. How are you?" Cassidy asked, taking Meade's hand and shaking it.

Meade beamed. "I'm really good. How are you?" She pointed. "Now, you work at Seaside Sweets with Marigold, is that right?"

"Yes, you've got a good memory."

Maya grabbed Meade's shoulders, presenting her to Cassidy. "Meade is brilliant. Like no joke."

"Maya," Meade said, giving her a warning glance and wiggling out of her sister's grasp.

"I'm just proud of you, okay?" Maya said, and Cassidy was starting to feel like she needed to step away.

A beefy guy Cassidy had seen at the Guppy a handful of times came up to them, handing Meade a glass of red wine. "Cabaret Sav…Sav…"

"Cabernet Sauvignon," Maya supplied.

"Whatever," he said. "Drunk juice." He laughed too hard as he smiled at Cassidy and Maya, looking for confirmation of his humor.

"Thank you," Meade said, taking the glass from him, her smile seeming to give him the affirmation he so desperately needed. The two of them moved into their own little world as they entered one another's personal spaces, smiling and doing the bar pickup dance.

Cassidy turned to Maya who was laser-focused on them, looking like a teacher at a middle school dance who needed to separate a preteen couple.

"Meade was just here for a visit a couple of months ago, wasn't she?" Cassidy asked.

Maya closed her eyes rubbing her temple. "She lives here now."

"Oh, wow. I had no idea. When did this happen?"

Maya glanced around and then moved in closer to Cassidy. "Three weeks ago. When she was here for her visit, I made the crucial error of talking to her about how upset I've been. I broke down with her, and as a result, she quit her job to come take care of me." She made quotes with her fingers and gave Cassidy a look. "I told you she would do this. I knew she would. I feel sick about it. If I would have just kept my big mouth shut…"

"Do you think that's really why she's here?" Cassidy asked.

Maya pursed her lips. "No. I think she was looking for any excuse to quit that job."

"What's she doing here for work?"

"She just got a job at a bar on the beach like she's freaking Tom Cruise in *Cocktail*. I swear, Cassidy, I don't know what else to do about her."

The guy said something and Meade giggled in response, laying her head on his shoulder.

Maya turned away. "I can't. I can't watch this. She's going to sleep with this guy. She's going to go home with this Neanderthal and have sex with him." Maya put her head in her hand.

Bo walked up and put his arm around Maya, gauging the scene. "Do you want me to get rid of him?" Bo asked.

"Yes," Maya said. Bo just lifted his eyebrows, and then Maya tightened her mouth into a wad. "No."

"Come on," Bo said. "Let's go over here and speak to Desiree and Ashe, okay?" Maya nodded and let herself be led off by her wonderful husband.

The piped-in music went down at the same time Kelly stood up on top of the bar. She whistled with her thumb and forefinger, and everyone turned to her. She cupped her hands over her mouth and shouted, "They just parked and are walking up to the back door now. Everybody…" She put a single finger up to her lips.

Everyone talked in hush tones while Cassidy's heart pounded. She wished like hell she wouldn't have come, but as she glanced around and saw Seanna, Blake, Maya, Bo, Marigold, Dane, Ethan, Ashe, and Desiree, she realized it would be pretty sorry if she wasn't there. She closed her eyes, thinking this would all be over in a matter of moments when she saw who he walked through the door with.

The sound of the door opening got her attention, and during that moment where everyone waited for Jesse to surface, Cassidy wondered if her body would ignite from nervous energy right then and there. A young woman with short, dark hair came through the door first, followed by a tall black man, with a blond girl after that, and then the crowd shouted, "Surprise!" as Jesse surfaced.

Cassidy had to hold onto her pounding heart to settle it, starting to seriously fear a heart attack. She was too damn old for new love. It was physically killing her.

"What?" Jesse said with a huge grin on his face. Cassidy had never seen him look happier, and he'd looked pretty damn happy when they were together.

Gracie held out both arms. "Welcome home, asshole!"

Everyone laughed and someone yelled, "Speech!"

"I can't form words, much less give a speech."

Gracie shoved him. "You can at least introduce your friends."

"Oh, I guess I could do that." His gaze went immediately to the blond girl, and Cassidy's heart plummeted. He motioned toward the girl. "This is Cara." He pointed at the guy. "That's Jousha and that's Devon." He glanced around. "I don't even know who the fuck all these people are."

Everyone laughed again, and someone yelled, "Fuck you, Jesse!"

He grinned and waved the guy off. "I do know who you are. You're all paying customers, or at least you better be." Everyone laughed again, and then as Jesse seemed to get his bearings, he clasped his hands together. "No, you all totally got me. I had no idea you were doing this. I've missed every one of you these past couple of months, which have been phenomenal. I met awesome new people and had an experience I'll always carry with me. I highly recommend doing it. Seriously. If you want to, come and talk to any of us and we'll hook you up with the right people to get involved."

People clapped, and Jesse looked embarrassed. He waved everyone off. "No, God, please don't clap for that. Just, everybody, I love you. If I had to come home, I'm glad it's to all you assholes." People shouted and clapped, and Jesse was brought in for a hug by someone at the front of the crowd.

The band started playing, and Cassidy rested on a barstool, trying to get her heartbeat back into step. Jesse had been transformed. Cassidy got it. Work like what he'd been doing made you into a new person. You appreciated life and people, and you became humble…at least most people did.

Cassidy shouldn't have been surprised to see him bring home a group of people. That kind of work drew people close and served to form lifelong friendships. And the way he looked at the blond woman, Cara, signaled to Cassidy that she'd gotten her wish. Jesse had found a woman his own age.

She didn't know if she was going to be able to stay. She needed to, just long enough to say hello and let him know she came. Although she couldn't think of anything more excruciating than facing him right then, his lovely new girl on his arm. Cassidy thought she might be sick.

Jesse and his new group of friends held court as people came by to say hello and hear about the work. Sebastian sidled up to her. "He's looking for you."

She rolled her eyes. "He doesn't remember I exist."

"I'm serious. He keeps peering around. He can't see you because you're sitting, but I guarantee you, he's trying to find you."

"You're high, Sebastian. He's with that blond girl."

"You don't know that."

"Have you seen how he looks at her?"

"What's in a look, huh?" She gave him one, and he held up a hand in concession. "I hear you. But seriously, he's with three people. You have no clue

who's who. For all you know he's with the guy."
Sebastian peered over at them. "God knows I'd like
to be with that guy."

She pinched his side with a smile.

"Hang on," Sebastian said as he waved and smiled
through gritted teeth. "He sees us."

Cassidy met Jesse's gaze from across the crowded
room and her heart leapt like a pole vaulter. She held
up a hand in a wave, and he gave her a serious,
resigned smile.

She waited for him to look away, and then she
stood. "Okay, I think I'm done here."

"You are not leaving here without speaking to
him."

Cassidy knew that was the right thing to do. She
just needed to get it over with. "Okay, let's go get in
line."

They made their way through the crowd of people
and waited while he finished up talking to some
people Cassidy didn't know. The young blonde was
right by Jesse's side, nodding politely and giving off
an air of confidence that Cassidy used to recognize
in herself before she let love make her insane.

Jesse met Cassidy's gaze and held up a finger
before going back to his guest, leaving her stomach
tied up in square knots.

When those people stepped away, Jesse turned to
Cassidy and Sebastian. He held out a hand to
Sebastian. "Hey, man. Thanks so much for coming."

Sebastian shook Jesse's hand. "Welcome back.
Looks like you've been missed." Sebastian glanced
around the room.

Jesse turned to Cassidy, his face flushed. "Hey."

She went in for a modest hug, trying not to drink in his touch, but it was really hard not to. She pulled away and gave him her warmest smile, willing her eyes not to water.

She turned to the blonde who was still by his side, and the young girl held out a hand. "I'm Cara."

Cassidy smiled at her. "Hi, Cara," she said, hoping she knew exactly how lucky she was to have landed on this particular trip with this man. "I'm Cassidy."

The girl stilled, her expression dropping for a moment, and then she smiled wide and gripped her hand harder. "I've heard so much about you."

"Oh," Cassidy said, taken off guard.

"Not just from Jesse, but from Andrea and Gregg."

"Oh my goodness," Cassidy said, the names of her friends from years past lighting her up. "They were on this trip with you all?" She shouldn't be surprised. It was very possible Noel and Ingrid had referred Jesse to their mutual friends.

"Yes, they were great. Everyone was. This was the first time I'd ever done something like this, but no one treated me like a newbie. No egos in sight."

Cassidy thought of Todd. He must not have been on this trip. She turned to Jesse. "What about you? How was your experience?"

"It was great. I don't think I'll ever be the same after it."

Cassidy nodded. "Then it was a success, for sure."

The group of them had an awkward silence, and it was Cara who saved them. "I hear you have a bakery in town."

Cassidy couldn't help but feel a little silly. "Yes, down the road a bit in Seaside. Where do you live?"

She tossed up her hands and looked at Jesse. "I'm sort of figuring that out."

Cassidy's heart plummeted. This was what she had wanted. She was getting her wish. Jesse had found someone his own age who seemed lovely and warm, and all the things he deserved.

Cara continued. "I graduated from Vandy in December, but I haven't really landed anywhere yet. I guess my stuff is in Nashville, but I'm still trying to figure out life."

"I can certainly understand that," Cassidy said.

Jesse smiled down at Cara so affectionately that Cassidy's heart crumbled like a sand castle.

Cassidy made a motion toward Jesse with a forced smile. "Well, welcome home."

"Thanks," he said, staring into her eyes with an expression she couldn't read, and didn't need to try to. Some people Cassidy didn't know were lurking behind her, ready to talk to Jesse. "We're going to head out. Enjoy the rest of your party."

His brow furrowed, mouth opened, but as Cassidy stepped aside, the people behind her swooped in, and once again, Jesse was hugging someone.

She gave Sebastian a look and they were headed toward the front door without a word to anyone else.

Chapter Twenty-Seven

Sebastian pulled up in the driveway to Cassidy's house. "Please, sweetie, let me come in. We'll watch some ridiculous trash TV and eat ice cream till we're sick or something."

She took his hand and squeezed it. "Thank you, but I really do want to be alone."

"Why, so you can sit around drawing up scenarios that may or may not even be legit?"

"I promise I won't do that. I'm just mentally exhausted. I want to go to bed, really."

He cocked his head to the side. "Really?"

She nodded.

"Okay, hon. But if you change your mind, I'm just a few miles away."

"I know. You're my saving grace. I love you."

"I love you, too, sweetie."

Cassidy headed inside and got ready for bed, but when she tried to get into it, she couldn't. She could feel him there in her bed for the past two months, but tonight, it seemed as empty as a casket.

She lay on the couch staring at the television but numb as a zombie. She'd done the right thing letting him go, but seeing the results of his trip had been more than she realized she was ready to handle. She'd started to wonder if she'd built the relationship up in her head more than it had truly been, but seeing him tonight, she knew she loved him more deeply than she'd let herself believe. Healing from the loss of him was going to be a long, rough journey.

At eleven, she finally decided she was going to need some help getting to sleep. Wine didn't even sound good, but surely she had an over-the-counter sleep aid in there somewhere. She'd rarely used those, but she wasn't sure how she was going to make it through this night without one. As she was searching for an expiration date on a bottle that probably pre-dated her move to Seaside, she stilled as a knock sounded on her front door.

Her phone dinged next, and she went for it, heart pounding. Jesse's name populated her screen, shooting a flame through her body.

It's me. I saw the television on.

She glanced over at the window by the door with the sheer curtains. He was right there on the other side of her door. Her heart beat so fast she had to hold her palm against it and still herself before she got it together. She took off her reading glasses, and then pulled her hair out of its bun letting it fall around her face, mussing it.

She clenched her eyes shut, readying herself for whatever was next, which could be anything. She's moving in with him. They're getting married. He's going back to live in Puerto Rico. Anything was possible.

She opened the door, and he met her gaze, looking contrite. The sight of him there at her doorstep practically made her dizzy with love. "Hey," he finally said.

"Hey."

"I'm sorry. I hope you weren't asleep."

"I wasn't. I was just…watching something."

He nodded. "Can I come in?"

"Oh," she said, feeling like an idiot. She opened the door. "Of course. Sorry, I'm a little out of it. It's late."

"I know. I'm sorry to bug you tonight, but I needed to see you."

She shut the door behind him and then proffered a hand toward the couch. "Can I get you anything?"

"No," he said, sitting down. "Thanks."

She sat on the couch, too, but farther away than usual. "How was the rest of your party?"

"I think it's still going on, but I got a hall pass because of the travel."

She nodded. "I didn't recognize too many of those people."

"They're mostly customers who I've gotten to know over the years. Your whole crew was there, I think…everyone who came on Chase and Shayla's wedding weekend."

"Yeah, I think they were all accounted for. They rarely miss a party."

He nodded. "It was humbling to have so many people come for me. I've felt humbled since the day

I got to Puerto Rico, actually."

"I know what you mean. Those trips can transform a person if you're not careful."

"Most definitely, in a lot of ways." He met her gaze, and she almost buckled from the weight of it.

She shifted in her seat. "So, you made some friends on the trip. That's awesome."

"Yeah, it was a really good time. I think I'll be tight with these guys forever. I know that sounds naïve, but—"

"It's not naïve. You probably will be. The bonds that can form on these volunteer trips can be forever binding. It's a wonderful thing," she said, begging the pressure at the backs of her eyes to loosen.

He frowned down at the couch. "I can see now how you got tight with that Todd guy in a situation like that."

The pit of her stomach churned. He could see, because he'd experienced that closeness with Cara. "Well, that's forever done," she said. "I'm sure of that now. Even the friendship part."

He looked up at her. "Really?"

"Yeah. He spoke to me in a way I'm not comfortable with that night we all went to dinner. I'd gotten whiffs of that behavior, but I'd chalked it up to stress. He does so much good for people, but when he doesn't get his way, he doesn't really have much grace about it."

He huffed. "I'm not sure I'm much better."

"You're not even in the same ballpark, Jesse."

He searched her gaze like he was looking for answers to something. She held it for as long as she could, and then glanced away. "Um, Cara seems lovely." It was time to get to the root of what was going on here. If he was going to break her heart, she was ready for the pain to start because hope could be a dangerous beast.

"She's fantastic. She just finished her degree in neuroscience. She may be one of the smartest people I've ever met."

Cassidy wasn't sure this could get much worse. *Better*, she thought. Better for him. "That's wonderful. Her brain probably needed a break after working so hard all those years."

He chuckled. "I guess so. School's no picnic, and I went to a state school."

She couldn't take her eyes off his neck, wanting nothing more than to have her mouth on it. She shook herself back to cold reality. "I'm really happy for you," she said, trying so hard to mean it, but her selfish heart made her a liar.

He frowned. "Cassidy, I'm not with Cara."

She blinked, hoping she'd heard him right. "No?" she asked, confused.

"God, no. She feels like a little sister to me. She's way too young for me."

Cassidy could not help but smile at this irony.

Jesse laughed, running a hand through his hair. "God, that was not how I meant for that to come out."

She let out a sigh to cleanse the soul, just smiling at him, her heart so full of battling emotions she was afraid a war was brewing inside of her.

He rested back on the couch. "I learned so much about myself on this trip. I know that sounds cliché."

"It's not cliché."

"This may sound hokey, but I don't think I've

taken any time to figure out who the real me is until now. I went from this super-structured, planned-out life with Lauren and her dad to this life here with my bar full of hookups and way too much drinking. The past several years have been a fuck-you to her and my brother. That's not me. That's not who I am."

She tucked her leg up under her. "Did this trip help you figure out who you are?"

He shrugged. "It was helpful, I think, but I'm not sure I'm there yet."

She smiled. "Join the club."

He met her gaze. "I visited Rachel a couple of months ago, after…" He averted his gaze down to his lap.

Cassidy's heart cinched. "Really? How did that go?"

"Good, I think. We talked about a lot. She's actually the one who encouraged me to do this trip, well, not directly, but in a way."

"That's great. I'm so glad you did it."

"I talked to her about what she said to you that day, why she brought up the miscarriage. I think it's more about me than it is you. She feels like she doesn't know who I am since I left my old life and did a one-eighty. And I'm not sure she's all that wrong."

Cassidy nodded, taking in his words at face value.

"I don't know who I was back then or who I was these past few years, but I know who I'm becoming since you've entered my life. I want to be happy. I don't want to carry around hate and resentment. I want to help people. I don't want to be selfish and so self-indulgent all the time. I want to be a man who will earn the love and trust of a woman as incredible as you are."

She smiled at him, the pull at her heart so strong she thought it might come right out of her chest.

He took her hand. "If you truly don't want to be with me, I can accept that. If you can say those words to me, that you want me to leave your life because a life with me isn't what you want, then I'll leave here tonight and I'll never bother you again. But if the real reason is because you feel some sort of guilt about taking away my opportunity for a family, or wanting me to have some sort of traditional life, that's not what I want. That's not what I wanted when I was twenty, but it was what I thought I had to do. And I almost married a woman who'd been cheating on me with my brother for years. Look what that life could have given me. When I think about a life with some woman I don't even know and kids and schools and corporate jobs because, let's face it, bartending isn't the ideal dad job...I don't want any of that. I didn't want it back then, and I don't want it now. I want you. I want a life where we love each other and travel together for both pleasure and working to help others. I want love and freedom and you." He took her arms and bore his gaze into hers. "I want you."

The tears streamed down her face before she even felt them coming. She swiped them away. "Jesse, I just need to be sure this is what you—"

His mouth was on hers and she reached for his neck, running her hands through his hair. He pulled away from her and had her tank top off in one big motion. He kissed her neck and her breasts, and then pulled away again, taking off his T-shirt. His tanned chest was the most beautiful site she'd ever seen, and she pushed him back on the couch, kissing a million different spots on it. She worked her way down, unbuttoning his shorts and pulling them off of him. She took him into her mouth with such urgency she had to make herself slow down so she didn't hurt him.

"Oh, fuck, Cassidy," he said, melting into the couch, eyes closed.

She pulled away, holding him in her hand. "I hate to ask this, because it isn't my business, but I really want you inside of me, and I need to know…do I need to go get a condom?" She held her breath while she waited for his answer.

He sat up and took her face into his hands. "You could have given me a bottle of blue pills, and I couldn't have gotten it up for another woman." She giggled at his wording, but his expression turned serious. "I know I fucked my way through my twenties, but when we do this, you and me, I get filled up inside like nothing I've ever known. I never want to be with another woman again."

She nodded and took his hands. "I never knew a love like this was possible. Thank you for letting me have it."

He buried his forehead into her neck. "Oh, God, Cassidy. I love you so much."

She clenched her eyes shut, drinking him in. She pulled him back from her and stared into his eyes. "I love you, too."

His smile made her heart dance a samba. She stood up and slid her shorts down then straddled him, taking him into her hand and guiding him inside of her. She moved on him, their eyes locked as his arms reached around her back, pulling her body close to him. She held onto the back of the couch as she moved on him, their bodies linked together as one. She wasn't sure there was a way to get any closer to him, and she never wanted to be apart from him again.

Chapter Twenty-Eight

"Damn, woman. You've gotten good at this," Jesse said, watching Cassidy balance on the paddleboard. "I thought you were afraid of the water."

"I was. I guess I still am, but I wanted to see your ocean like you see it out here," she said, watching her feet as they adjusted on the board.

Goddamn he wanted to kiss her right now. He probably could, but he didn't want to scare her. She'd done something for him, learning how to paddleboard while he was gone, and he wasn't going to push his luck.

This life with her was what he never knew he'd been searching for. But here he was with her. He hadn't been sure he could do it, but he'd somehow convinced her to trust him and to believe that she was what he wanted. This life with her was everything to him and a world more.

She gazed out into the vast ocean. "This ocean of

yours isn't bad."

"Yeah?" he said with a grin.

"Yeah. It's pretty breathtaking."

He gazed at her. "Mmm hmm."

She smiled over at him. "What are you looking at?"

He grinned. "Nothing."

She smiled down at her feet. "I'm gonna be a tightrope walker before this is through."

"You could. You about ready to head back in?"

"I'm kind of enjoying it out here."

"You wouldn't rather come back out on the boat?"

"Oh God yes," she said, maneuvering herself around toward the shore. He smiled the whole way back in.

They walked their boards back to his bar and stacked them together on the rack he'd installed to hold both. It was goofy, but he loved seeing them there together.

He turned to her with a kiss. "I love you."

"I love you, too," she said, now free with her *I love yous*. It'd been a tough road to get there, but she was open now with her feelings. She'd gone all-in, it seemed, allowing herself to be with him. He pulled her to him, hands resting possessively on her ass. "Want to detour upstairs for a minute?"

"A minute? That's all you've got for me now?"

He squeezed her ass. "A day? Hell, a week?"

She kissed him. "I was promised a boat ride."

He kissed her back, walking her in a circle. "Mmm, okay. Let me get the keys from my office."

They headed to the bar area, and as she parted from him to go to the ladies room, they mouthed, "I love you," to one another. God, he knew he was getting exhausting for anyone who witnessed his PDA with her.

He opened the drawer and grabbed his keys along with the black box he'd had the past three days. He knew this was a humongous risk, and he was probably chancing his good luck, but he couldn't stop himself no matter how hard he tried. He was ready for this. When he'd thought about marrying Lauren, he used to get hives. But when he thought about marrying Cassidy, he got nothing but a rush of happiness that couldn't be contained.

Cassidy stared out at the ocean. She'd never spent so much time on the water or, heck, even outside. But Jesse made her want to experience life. She'd thought she'd lived a lot with as much travel as she'd done, but she hadn't even started yet. Living was sharing an ocean with the man she loved. Living was the way her heart pounded when she saw him after they'd been apart even for a workday. Living was allowing herself to be happy with him.

He messed around in the cooler and then handed her a seltzer water. "Thanks," she said with a smile.

"What are you smiling at?" he asked, sitting next to her.

"I'm just happy."

He stared at her, his blue eyes searching hers. His head dropped down as if he was in thought, and then he met her gaze, taking her hands. "You've changed my life, Cassidy. You've made me a whole person again. I was bitter and floundering around without any focus or semblance of a meaningful life, and you've made me into a person I'm okay with looking in the mirror at."

"You did that Jesse, not me."

"I did that because of you." He kissed her knuckles and then released a deep breath. "I don't want to live another minute of my life without you." He dropped her hands and turned around, lifting up the seat beside him, and then he turned back toward her, dropping to kneel in front of her.

Cassidy's heart expanded in her chest like a balloon, thumping like a bass drum.

He opened the box to display a diamond ring she couldn't dream of focusing on. He took her hand. "Will you marry me, Cassidy?"

She covered her mouth with a shaky hand, staring at the ring which was vintage and unassuming but one of the most beautiful sights she'd ever seen. "Jesse," was all she could say, and it came out in a high-pitched whisper.

He rested the box on her knee, and his other hand on her thigh. "I swear I will spend every day of my life making you happy."

She scratched the back of her head, staring at the ring, her whole body quivering. There were a million reasons to say no. He was too young. She was too old. They couldn't have a baby together. She'd spend a lifetime feeling like she'd cheated him out of another life. But her heart was so full of love for this unbelievable man who'd dropped into her life and shaken her to a reality that felt like a dream. But he was real, and was hers, and selfish as it may be, she couldn't let him go...not again.

She pressed her palm against her forehead,

desperately trying to hold back her smile. "Jesse, are you sure about this?"

He dropped his head into her lap. "Oh my God, woman. Do you not see that I'm freaking mad over you?"

She played with his hair. "We could just move in together."

He lifted his head up to face her and then sat down next to her. "I don't want to just move in. I want you to be my wife. I want to commit my life to you. I want us to move forward together and I don't want this bullshit in the back of your mind about me possibly leaving one day for some other life I don't want and will never want. I want you. I want us. And I want us to be married. We can have a long engagement if you want, but I want commitment, not only to you, but from you."

It dawned on her for the first time that he might be afraid she would change her mind and want a different life. She couldn't fathom a life without him. She squeezed his knee. "I do have one thing I'd like to talk to you about first." His brow furrowed in concentration at her words and she swallowed hard before moving forward. "Even though I don't want to have a baby at my age, one thing I have thought about doing at some point, even before I met you…and this would be sometime a bit into the future…but I've thought about fostering. If we did get married and built a life together, would that be something you would consider doing with me?"

"Wow," he said, looking off at the ocean. Her stomach plummeted. Had she just messed all this up? He turned back to her. "That's really something you've wanted?"

"It's something I've thought about. I haven't been ready though, and I'm still not to be honest. But I think if I had someone to co-parent with, the idea of it would become a lot less daunting. And I wouldn't want a baby. I'd be more comfortable with an older child, or maybe a couple of older children. I don't know. We'd have to figure it out as we went. But do you have thoughts about that?"

He shrugged. "I think it would be really hard and really rewarding. It might be perfect for us."

She smiled at him, shaking her head. "You really are the most wonderful man. Do you know this about yourself?"

He moved her hair over her shoulder with one finger, brushing her neck, making her insides melt. "So?"

She closed her eyes, the *no* that should be on the tip of her tongue somewhere off in the vast distance. "Yes, I'd love to marry you, Jesse."

The shock on his face almost made her a little nervous. Had he changed his mind?

"You will?" he asked like he couldn't believe it.

She giggled. "Yes. Does the offer still stand?"

He put his head in his hands for a moment and then lifted up with a grin on his face like she'd never seen, making her heart practically fly out of her chest. "I wasn't sure you'd say yes."

"Are you crazy?" she asked.

"Really?" he asked.

She wiggled her fingers at him. "Yes, give me that beautiful ring."

He slid it onto her finger, and it fit perfectly. "I

stole one of your other rings I've seen you wear on that finger and took it with me when I got this."

She shook her head. "God, I'm a lucky girl."

She held her hand up in front of her, staring at this new ring, this new life she was headed into.

"That looks so good on you," he said.

She turned to him. "Thank you, Jesse. Thank you for so much." She could feel the tears coming, but this time she wanted to let them flow.

He wiped them away with his thumbs, searching her gaze. "I'm the thankful one."

The Next Chapter

Meade stood in the living room of a home in Alys Beach that may have been the most expensive house she would ever step foot in. This art party, which to Meade felt more like a gallery showing, was being sponsored by a couple named Gwendolen and Rob. Apparently, they threw Halloween and Christmas parties to thrill the masses of 30A and had address books thicker than some small cities' phone books.

Good for Desiree and Marigold, who were a team of artist and agent who seemed to be pretty unstoppable. Meade would definitely be buying a piece if she ever banked any money…which was fairly unlikely, actually. 30A wasn't cheap, but she'd found a long-term rental that her bartender gig would support as long as she worked plenty of shifts, if you could call pouring drinks on a beach work.

A server stepped up to her with a tray of wine glasses. She took a glass of white with a smile. He was hot, though at least ten years younger, not that she ever let that stand in her way. "Thanks so much. Hope you're not working too hard."

He smiled back. "Hardly working's more like it."

"Ah, in that case," she said as she held up her glass with her best *come get me* eyes, "cheers." She indicated the tray, daring him to take a drink.

He glanced down at the tray and then around the room, locking eyes with the lady who appeared to be the head caterer who gave him a stern shake of her head. He met Meade's gaze. "I can't right now."

"I hope you can later," she said, eyeing him up and down. Oh, how she loved the thrill of the chase.

He grinned. "I think I can."

"That's the spirit."

Maya, her buzzkill of a sister, sidled up beside her, taking a glass off the tray. "Thank you so much," she said in the tone of a dismissal, which had the cutie scurrying away.

Meade exhaled a deep breath and glanced around the living room with its glass walls and view of an infinity pool with the ocean as a backdrop. "I think I'll take this as my next house."

"It's not like you couldn't have this if you really wanted it."

Meade had to work hard not to roll her eyes with regard to her sister's nonstop comments about her life choices. For whatever reason, Maya had taken on the challenge of fixing Meade, which hadn't worked out too well for her to date.

"Well, I guess for now I'll just have to settle for my efficiency of a rental, which is lovely, by the way."

"I didn't say it wasn't."

Meade turned to her sister. "Wanna go outside by the pool, or can you take the heat?"

Maya peered out at the pool. "It is pretty hot out there."

"I'm built for heat," Meade said and then slipped away from her suffocating sister.

As she stepped out onto the pool deck, the July heat beat down on her like a punishment. She was getting used to the heat. She worked in it every day. But there was definitely a difference between sporting a tank top and shorts under a pavilion with a fan blowing, and being in it wearing a fancy dress with heels. Meade didn't mind being grimy at work. At an elegant party, she minded a little. But she wouldn't turn back now after she shamed her sister about not coming.

She stood staring out at the ocean wondering why she waited so long to come down here. Chicago was freaking freezing in the winter. She'd grown up in Indy, so she was no stranger to the cold, but it didn't mean she'd ever gotten used to it. She'd have followed Maya down here the second she'd made the decision to move for Bo. But clueless as Meade could be in her relationships, she knew to give the two of them space while they figured their way forward. They were an old married couple now though, and Maya was trying unsuccessfully to get and stay pregnant. Meade's heart broke for her sister and her struggles. She just wanted to be near Maya even though she drove her crazy.

"Hot enough for you," came a man's voice from behind her. She turned around to find a guy about her age as dressed up as she was.

She turned back toward the ocean. "I like the heat."

He held out a hand. "I'm Ryder."

She blinked, the name taking her off guard. He didn't seem like a *Ryder* for some reason.

"I know, I probably look more like an Alex or a Felix or something like that. I think my mom hoped I'd grow up to ride a Harley and wear a motorcycle jacket." He gave her a smile, or more like a little smirk, with just one side of his mouth.

She took his hand and shook it, getting a good look at him. He had a Clark Kent thing going on. Nerdy as hell, but probably cute somewhere underneath his glasses. "Meade," she said, giving no further explanation.

He smiled. "Nice to meet you, Meade. Are you a friend of Gwendolen and Rob's?"

"No, I'm an acquaintance of the artist."

"Oh, really? I go way back with Desiree."

This was a surprising turn of events. Desiree, who reminded Meade of Zoe Kravitz and was as chill and enigmatic, did not seem like the kind of person who would go way back with this chatty guy.

"You do?" Meade asked.

"Yeah. We went to high school together in New Orleans. When I moved here I heard she was living here too, so I looked her up."

That made a little more sense, though this guy did not strike Meade as the New Orleans type.

"What brought you here?" she asked, a little curious, but not too much.

"The ocean. I'm a marine biologist. I'm studying

the long-term effects of the Deepwater Horizon oil spill of 2010."

"Mmm," she said with a nod, glancing around. She hoped Maya wouldn't see her talking to this guy. This was just exactly the type of man Maya would squeal over. Meade didn't go for guys with brains. Sure, she was cerebral, but that was a part of her life she compartmentalized, and for very good reason.

"I've seen you before, actually," he said.

She gave him a sideways glance. "Excuse me?"

"At the library. I volunteer there." He pointed at her. "*The Excellent Doctor Blackwell: The Life of the First Woman Physicia*n."

This was creepy. That was a book she'd read at the library last week. It wasn't even like he checked it out for her because she didn't have a library card since she wasn't a real resident.

She jerked a thumb over her shoulder. "I'm gonna head back inside."

He held up both hands. "I'm sorry. That was probably weird. I promise I wasn't stalking you. It's just that you dropped it off in the cart to be re-shelved right as I was walking up to it, so I just sort of noticed it. I like to see what people are interested in reading."

She gauged him. Maybe he wasn't creepy. He was definitely cute, but she didn't do nerdy, and this guy was for sure a nerd.

"Okay," she said, glancing inside to see what that server was up to—flirting with another girl, of course. Rats.

"Well, I just thought I'd say hi. I'm going back inside." He waved and headed off before she had the chance to protest. Not that she was planning on doing so, but with the hottie waiter otherwise occupied, she might have at least talked to him a minute. She watched through the glass window as he met up with Desiree inside, and she wrapped her arm around him, giving him a kiss on the cheek. Maybe he was cuter than she'd originally thought.

Nah, he wasn't her type.

To stay informed of Melissa's new releases, bonus content, and giveaways, sign up for her newsletter at melissachambers.com.

If you enjoyed this story, please consider leaving a review on Amazon. Even a really short review is very much appreciated!

Will Ryder finally be the one to settle Meade's restless heart?
Rosemary Beach Kisses coming soon!

Seaside Sweets, Seacrest Sunsets, *Seagrove Secrets,* and *WaterColor Wishes* now available on Amazon

Acknowledgments

When I started this series, it was never my intention to write Cassidy's story. I thought she would make a great *wise old owl* confidant for the younger characters in this series. But by far, Cassidy's story has been the most requested by readers (with Sebastian coming in second. I hear you on Sebastian!).

I loved the mystery Cassidy had about her in the previous books, so when I first sat down to expose her inner emotions through her story, I was a bit intimidated. But I could not believe how fast this story flew off my fingertips. It was such an immense joy to write, so I want to thank all of you who encouraged me to tackle the task of giving Cassidy her happily ever after.

Once again, a huge hug and thank you to Kristen Kovach, one of the busiest people I know, who always finds time to give me a thoughtful beta read. You are such a treasure to me both as a reader and as a friend.

Big thanks to Sid Grimes for being such a good sport with my very strange research questions, and a warm thank you Gina Kelley for providing inspiration for the Jamaica portion of this story.

Thanks as always to my editor Trish Milburn who always leads me in the right direction.

Thank you to Kat O'Nell and Marianne Donley for getting me up at the crack of dawn on Saturday mornings to keep at this! To AJ Scudiere and Shannon Brown for sharing their vast knowledge of the publishing industry. And to the talented Monica McCabe who always helps me tweak my blurbs. Through the Music City Romance Writers, I have truly surrounded myself with wonderful, supportive people.

Thank you to my adviser and dear friend Jessica Calla who helps me figure out all the stuff, and to Greg Howard who devotedly listens while I tell him all the stuff Every. Single. Day.

And most of all, thank you to my guys. Our little family is more precious to me than either of you could ever conceive. I love the two of you and our sweet Marlene around the world and back.

About the Author

Melissa Chambers writes contemporary novels for young, new, and actual adults. A Nashville native, she spends her days working in the music industry and her nights tapping away at her keyboard. While she's slightly obsessed with alt rock, she leaves the guitar playing to her husband and kid. She never misses a chance to play a tennis match, listen to an audiobook, or eat a bowl of ice cream. (Rocky road, please!) She's a member of RWA and has served as the president for the Music City Romance Writers.

Made in United States
North Haven, CT
20 July 2022

21627322R00178